'You don't
further?'

She stared num... burning her cheeks. 'N-not now,' she s...

'What are you afraid of? It's not like you.'

Capri tried to smile, but her lips trembled. 'Isn't it? I wouldn't know.'

'You don't remember ever making love?'

'No,' she admitted. 'I suppose that seems silly, when you…'

Her voice trailed off. He knew her intimately, had done for more than two years.

'No…it's not silly,' Rolfe said. 'Kind of bizarre, but I find it rather intriguing.'

Daphne Clair lives in Aotearoa, New Zealand, with her Dutch-born husband. Their five children have left home but drift back at irregular intervals. At eight years old she embarked on her first novel, about taming a tiger. This epic never reached a publisher, but metamorphosed male tigers still prowl the pages of her romances. Daphne is the author of over fifty romance titles and her other writing includes non-fiction, poetry and short stories. She has won literary prizes in New Zealand and America.

Recent titles by the same author:

RECKLESS ENGAGEMENT
SUMMER SEDUCTION

WIFE TO
A STRANGER

BY
DAPHNE CLAIR

MILLS & BOON®

DID YOU PURCHASE THIS BOOK WITHOUT A COVER?

If you did, you should be aware it is **stolen property** as it was reported *unsold and destroyed* by a retailer. Neither the author nor the publisher has received any payment for this book.

All the characters in this book have no existence outside the imagination of the author, and have no relation whatsoever to anyone bearing the same name or names. They are not even distantly inspired by any individual known or unknown to the author, and all the incidents are pure invention.

All Rights Reserved including the right of reproduction in whole or in part in any form. This edition is published by arrangement with Harlequin Enterprises II B.V. The text of this publication or any part thereof may not be reproduced or transmitted in any form or by any means, electronic or mechanical, including photocopying, recording, storage in an information retrieval system, or otherwise, without the written permission of the publisher.

This book is sold subject to the condition that it shall not, by way of trade or otherwise, be lent, resold, hired out or otherwise circulated without the prior consent of the publisher in any form of binding or cover other than that in which it is published and without a similar condition including this condition being imposed on the subsequent purchaser.

MILLS & BOON and MILLS & BOON with the Rose Device are registered trademarks of the publisher.

*First published in Great Britain 1998
Harlequin Mills & Boon Limited,
Eton House, 18-24 Paradise Road, Richmond, Surrey TW9 1SR*

© Daphne Clair de Jong 1998

ISBN 0 263 81207 3

*Set in Times Roman 10½ on 12 pt.
01-9810-47911 C1*

*Printed and bound in Norway
by AiT Trondheim AS, Trondheim*

CHAPTER ONE

IT WAS a small room. The man standing at the window with his back to her looked big by contrast. His broad shoulders hunched slightly under a crumpled white linen shirt, and his hands were thrust into the pockets of navy trousers, tautening the fabric over lean hips.

From the bed she could see only a washed-denim sky, the pale, peeling trunk of a gum tree, and a dusting of opaque clouds between the green cotton curtains. She wondered what he was looking at.

Pulling her gaze from him, she examined the room. There was a hard-looking tan leather chair, with a burgundy tie draped carelessly over its back as though the man had discarded it there some time ago. On the plain cream wall opposite the bed hung a cheap print of an English country cottage. A white-painted locker by her bed held a water jug and a glass.

It was a hospital room.

Perhaps she made some faint sound, or he heard a stirring of the bedclothes. The man turned, starkly silhouetted against the light from outside.

'Capri,' he said, his voice deep and unsurprised. 'So you decided to come back.'

'Back?'

Her voice sounded strange, scarcely more than an uncertain whisper in the quiet of the room.

Taking his hands from his pockets, the man crossed the narrow space to the bed. 'To the land of the living. You've been out for some time.'

'Out.'

His quickly checked movement might have denoted impatience. 'Unconscious. Do you remember what happened to you?'

She started to shake her head, winced. 'No.'

He leaned forward a little—brown, enigmatic eyes raking her face, a strand of nearly-black hair falling onto his forehead. 'I'll call a nurse.'

He reached across her, finding the electric signal button with a decisive thumb. A whiff of his masculine scent entered her nostrils, a mixture of warmth, soap, sweat and shirting. She saw he hadn't shaved lately; his cheeks were fuzzed with shadowy growth.

One hand on the metal bed frame behind her, he paused, his face only inches from hers, his nostrils flaring as if he in turn had been caught by her scent. She looked into his eyes, dark and lustrous, with gold flecks about the irises. His mouth, firm and hard despite the generously chiselled curve of the lower lip, momentarily quirked at one corner, and then he withdrew, standing tall and aloof and thrusting his hands back into his pockets.

She took an unsteady breath, and her parched lips began to frame a question, but then a woman in a white uniform came hurrying on rubber soles, and made for the bedside. 'Well, well. So you've finally woken up!'

The nurse's fingers closed about her wrist, found the pulse. 'How are you feeling?'

'Not...so good.'

The man moved again, very slightly. The nurse studied her watch as she counted, then placed the hand she held back on the coverlet. 'You've been knocked about a bit. But we'll soon have you right as rain.'

'Knocked about—how?'

The woman studied her with a shrewd professional gaze. 'You don't remember?'

This time she was careful not to shake her head, but before she could get the words out the question was answered for her in a curt masculine voice. 'She doesn't. And I think she has a headache.'

The nurse's eyes lifted to him, then returned to her patient. 'You had a nasty whack on the head,' she explained cheerfully. 'Plus bruising and mild hypothermia. How bad is the headache?'

'It only hurts when I move.' She felt languid, every word an effort.

'Can you tell me your name?'

'My name?' She blinked.

'Her name's Capri Helene Massey.' He was definitely impatient this time. 'If you people hadn't known it, you wouldn't have been able to get hold of me.'

The nurse glanced up. 'It's standard practice to check after a concussion, Mr Massey,' she said calmly. 'Just in case there's been some damage.'

'Sorry. I'm not familiar with medical procedure.' After the curt apology he retreated again to the window.

'When were you born?' The nurse returned to her inquisition.

Automatically she recited her birth-date.

'Good. And do you know what year this is?'

Again the answer was easy, requiring no thought.

'Do you remember your present address?'

Panic gripped her, making her temples cold, her breathing irregular. 'I...I'm not sure...'

The nurse looked across her, raising her brows at the silent man who now came back to the bed. He said, 'She's been moving about lately.'

The nurse patted her hand. 'You might have a bit of

a memory gap—it's not unusual. Do you remember this gentleman here?' Smiling up at him.

'Well, Capri?' he said when she didn't answer immediately. His voice held irony. 'Have you forgotten me?'

'You're Rolfe,' she said clearly, positively. 'Rolfe Massey.'

He nodded. 'Your husband.' He didn't smile, although he was looking at her.

The nurse said encouragingly, 'You recognise him. Well, that's all right.'

He lifted his head. 'Satisfied?'

The woman beamed at him. 'You'll be relieved. The doctor will check her over again, though, and tell you if we need to keep her for another day or two.'

'Right. Thanks.' He nodded dismissively, and after a moment's hesitation the nurse left.

Rolfe seemed to be studying the pattern on the bed-cover. When he raised his eyes again they appeared almost black. 'I suppose it wasn't for lack of trying,' he said.

'What?' She stared at him. 'I'm sorry?'

His gaze narrowed, and his head jerked sharply as if he'd sensed something unexpected in the air, but the movement was quickly checked. 'It doesn't matter,' he said. 'You're not well enough for this discussion.' There was a short pause, and then he said on an oddly intense note, 'Shall I take you home, Capri? Is that what you'd like?'

Home. The word conjured up warmth, comfort—love. 'Of course,' she said, and saw a startling flare of some potent, primitive emotion in his eyes. 'As soon as the doctor says it's all right.' She had the feeling that if

she'd said, *Yes—now*, he'd have picked her up and bun-
dled her off with him then and there.

As it was, he took a breath that lifted the fabric of his
shirt for seconds before he audibly released it. 'Of
course,' he echoed her. 'I meant...when they've cleared
you.'

Her eyelids drooped, and he said, 'You look tired...
darling. Why don't you go to sleep?'

She should be asking questions, like what had happened to her, and what her last address had been, and
why...why...

Thinking was too difficult. She drifted, thought she
felt her hand taken in a large, warm one, and another
kind of warmth, bristly and underlaid with hard bone,
briefly rubbed against the back of it. Then she slept.

When she woke Rolfe was gone. A different nurse took
her pulse, read her blood pressure, poked a thermometer
into her mouth, and later other people bustled about her
with charts and stethoscopes, asked how she felt, and
gently prodded and kneaded her body, which was tender
with bruises.

They told her that New South Wales had been lashed
by spring storms, and a landslip caused by heavy rain
had derailed a train, sending several carriages sliding
into the Hunter River. She'd been lucky. Some of the
other passengers were on the critical list in this hospital,
the nearest to the crash site, while a few needing specialist care had been flown to Sydney. She'd had a brain
X-ray on admission, and later a CT scan because she
had been taking her time to come round, but they had
shown no cause for concern.

'Anything worrying you?' someone asked at last.

She looked at him gratefully. 'The nurse said...I might have memory gaps.'

The doctor nodded. 'That's right. You don't remember the accident?'

'It's not only the accident I don't remember.'

'Oh?' He sounded almost casual. 'How much have you lost?'

It was a relief to confide in someone. 'I think...an awful lot.'

Another doctor came, shone lights in her eyes, and asked more questions, some of them general, others personal. At the end of it all he assured her again that there was no sign of physical damage, suggested she rest and try not to worry, and departed looking thoughtful.

She begged to be allowed to shower, and a nurse was detailed to monitor her.

'Not much of an end to your holiday,' the woman commented, 'getting involved in that crash.'

'No.' She took the soap the nurse handed her and stepped into the blessed warmth of the shower.

Afterwards, her wet hair wrapped in a towel, she caught a glimpse of herself in the mirror over the bathroom basin and was reassured at the familiarity of jade-green eyes fringed by thick, dark lashes, and a slightly long but straight nose in an oval face. Her skin was too pale and her lips bloodless and cracked, but apart from that she looked herself.

Shivering despite the steamy fug of the bathroom, she wished she felt it.

Just showering had exhausted her, and she was too listless to read the magazines a nurse found for her, instead staring out the window at a view of low tawny hills and, nearer, the gum tree with its narrow leaves twisting in the yellow sunlight.

Rolfe returned bearing roses and carnations in sparkling florist's wrap, and a parcel that he told her was toiletries he'd been advised by the nursing staff to buy for her. He had shaved and changed into jeans and a casual shirt.

The bouquet filled her arms, and perhaps that was why he didn't kiss her. His glance was sharply enquiring. 'How are you feeling?'

She inhaled the scent of the flowers. 'The headache's gone.'

'Good.' Walking round to take the tan chair between the bed and the window, he sat down and leaned forward, his clasped hands between spread knees, but then shifted back, coolly surveying her. 'You still look... fragile.'

She gave him a cautious smile. 'That's how I feel. What about you?'

He arched a black brow at her. 'Me?'

'You weren't with me in the train?'

'No.'

His face looked hollowed about the freshly shaved cheeks, his eyes tired, and he had a taut air of strain, as if he couldn't relax.

She said, 'I suppose I gave you a fright, getting hurt, and then...you've been waiting for me to wake up. Since yesterday, they said.'

He shrugged absently. 'I'm just glad you did wake. They told me you would, but...'

'So am I,' she said softly, 'glad.' She removed one hand from the flowers and stretched it towards him. 'Thank you for being with me.'

Rolfe hesitated before placing his fingers over hers,

holding them. His gaze stayed on their linked hands. 'I couldn't not come,' he said.

'Of course. You're my husband.'

He looked up then, his eyes scanning her face. She moved to stretch her other hand to him, somehow needing that warm personal contact, and the flowers slipped, rolling down to the side of the bed.

Rolfe rescued them and stood up, releasing her. 'I'll see if I can rustle up a vase or something,' he promised, and left the room.

He returned with a big glass vase that he filled with water from the room basin, plunging the bouquet straight into it.

'They're lovely,' she said. 'Thank you.'

He looked down at her and his hand lifted almost as though he couldn't help it, his knuckles lightly brushing her cheek as he fingered her hair that had dried to a thick honey-brown bob with lighter streaks, the ends just level with her earlobes. 'Suits you,' he murmured.

She reached up to clasp his hand, but already he had withdrawn it.

'They said after you woke that if there are no obvious problems you may be discharged tomorrow,' he said. 'The accident has stretched the hospital's resources. Do you want me to book us into a hotel for a day or two, or shall we fly straight back to New Zealand?'

'New Zealand?'

'You did say you wanted to come home.' His voice had turned gravelly. 'Or have you changed your mind?'

'I haven't changed my mind.' The reply was automatic. Her heart thudded uncomfortably. She turned her head, staring out of the window, where darkness was creeping over the hills.

He said, 'You do know you're in Australia, don't you?'

'Of course I do.' She looked back at him.

'So where were you staying?'

She opened her mouth to reply, then paused. Finally she said, 'You must know that.'

He was gazing at her curiously. 'You don't remember.'

'No.'

'Do you remember anything that's happened to you in the past two months?'

'No...I don't.' She moistened her lips and said huskily, 'I seem to have forgotten...most of my life.'

Rolfe stared down at her, his eyes going nearly black. 'You knew me when you woke.'

Rolfe. She had known him, known his name. Just as she had known her birth-date without having to think. It had been reassuring, that familiarity. 'Yes, I recognised you.'

'How much do you remember about...us? About our life together?'

She looked away, running her tongue across her lips. 'I knew your face,' she confessed finally. 'Your name. That's all.'

'That's all?' Rolfe repeated.

She said helplessly, 'I know that must be a shock.'

He gazed down at her with frowning speculation. 'And now?' he enquired. 'Has anything more come to mind?'

'No.'

This time there was a lengthy silence, as if he had trouble taking that in. 'If you don't remember anything about me,' he said slowly at last, 'anything about our marriage, then for all intents and purposes I'm a stranger to you.'

'Yes,' she agreed, her hands twisting painfully together on the bedcover. 'Yes, you are. A total stranger.'

CHAPTER TWO

'WHAT exactly do you remember?' Rolfe demanded.

She swallowed. 'Not much. I remember things when I'm asked directly, or when something reminds me…'

His mouth compressed and his cheeks grew taut. 'Do the doctors know this?'

'They say it's probably temporary. And I feel fine, really…just a bit tired.'

Rolfe regarded her broodingly. 'I'll talk to them.'

'They've already examined me thoroughly. I just need to be…home.' In familiar surroundings where she was safe and loved. Then surely this surreal feeling of existing in a vacuum would be dispelled. All she needed was the right trigger to fill the inexplicable void.

'Still…' Rolfe looked at a loss. That probably didn't happen to him often. He had the air of a man who knew his way around his world. 'I'll be back,' he said abruptly, swung round and left the room.

When he came back she'd been dozing. He leaned down to kiss her cheek, said he'd leave her to sleep and was gone.

Throughout the night she was dimly aware of being regularly checked on, and in the morning she was examined by a neurologist, then sent for another scan and more tests because Rolfe, she was told, had insisted.

Late in the day the neurologist told her, 'The good news is, all the tests have come up negative. A knock on the head can do strange things to people, but the amnesia is probably temporary. Your husband says you want to go home, back to New Zealand?'

'Um...yes...' Aware that she sounded less than positive, she said more firmly, 'Yes, I do.'

He smiled. 'Of course.'

She repeated her theory that familiar surroundings would surely solve the puzzling problem of her memory.

'You're probably right,' he agreed. 'Take it easy for a little while, and don't try to force anything. I'll give you a letter for your own doctor. If things don't start coming back to you spontaneously pretty soon, you'd better see someone.'

When she asked about her belongings, the nurse said, 'We gave your shoulder bag to your husband for safety. Your passport and money are there, but your makeup is in the locker. Things were a bit wet but there didn't seem to be much damage. The police sent along a box of passengers' effects soon after you came in, stuff that had been found in the wreckage, and we identified you from your passport photo.'

Next day Rolfe brought in a stack of wrapped parcels and shopping bags, put them on the bed and began opening them. 'They tell me if I look after you I can take you home. I bought three bras—I hope one of them fits.'

'I don't have any clothes?' she queried.

'The ones you were wearing were ruined. Even the undies were pretty bedraggled, and one bra strap was broken. You may have had a suitcase but it hasn't been found. And as you don't know where you were staying...'

'But don't *you*? Weren't we together?'

He gave her a quick look. 'No, we weren't.'

She'd assumed that they'd been holidaying together,

that she'd only been on a short trip without him, perhaps shopping or visiting someone. 'Where were you?'

'In New Zealand. I came as soon as I could get a flight. Look...' he touched her arm '...why don't you get dressed and we can talk properly later?'

'All right.' She looked at the things scattered on the bed, some still in their wrappings.

'Do you want some help?' he asked her. He reached out to undo the tie on her hospital gown.

'No!' She shook her head. 'No, thanks.'

Still she hesitated, and after a moment he said, 'I'll...go and see if I can find the charge nurse.'

She picked up a bra—cream satin and lace. When she eased it on and did up the hooks it fitted quite well. She found matching panties, then shook out a jade-green cotton dress, low-necked with tiny front buttons and a gently flared skirt. She slipped the dress on and found it an easy fit.

A smart-looking boutique bag with handles and a zipper-type closure contained a primrose-yellow lined cotton jacket that she didn't think she'd need.

Rolfe had even bought dark green soft shoes with a medium wedge heel. And stockings and a suspender belt that she looked at with faint surprise. The sun was shining outside, giving no hint of the recent storms, and she decided to go bare-legged.

She unzipped the makeup bag that had been in her locker, applied sunscreening foundation, used soft olive shadow on her eyelids, touched a mascara wand to the tips of her lashes, and coloured her pale lips a warm coral.

Among the bags and wrappings she'd almost missed a small tissue-wrapped box, containing a phial of perfume. She was applying some to her inner wrist when Rolfe tapped on the door and then came in.

'Thank you.' She lifted her wrist to sniff at the slightly musky scent. 'You thought of everything.'

'Even your favourite perfume.'

'Really?' She dabbed the scent on her other wrist, then behind her ears, before she stoppered the bottle.

'You missed a spot.'

'What?'

Rolfe walked over to her and said, 'You usually put some here.' A lean finger touched the shallow little valley between her breasts, and his eyes darkened as her startled gaze flew to his face.

He quickly withdrew his hand. 'You look nice,' he said. 'The dress fits.'

'Yes.' She could still feel the intimate imprint of his finger on her skin.

She put away the bottle and moved to gather up the wrappings on the bed. 'I only tried one bra. Do you want to return the others to the shop?'

'No.' He slanted her a look of amused surprise. 'You may be able to wear them later. They're all the same size.' He stuffed the used wrappings into the rubbish bag near the basin while she folded the spare bras into the boutique bag along with the unused stockings and suspender belt.

She said, 'They told me you have my shoulder bag and passport.'

'In the hire car with my things. All your ID was in there, including a medical card listing me as your next of kin.'

After they entered the car he handed her the shoulder bag. The soft honey-coloured leather was stained with muddy water-marks.

'I'm afraid it's rather the worse for wear,' Rolfe commented. 'I've dried everything out, but some stuff was beyond saving. Fortunately your passport was zipped into the inner pocket and didn't come off too badly.'

As they left the car park she opened up the bag and went through the contents. The lining was still damp and smelled musty. Several credit cards were tucked into a card pocket, and she found a silver ballpoint pen, a Bank of New Zealand chequebook looking sadly crinkled, two keys on a ring, and a coin-purse containing Australian money, the notes crumpled but dry.

In the centre pocket of the bag she discovered a slim flower-patterned plastic folder designed for two photographs, and opened it to see her own face as a child looking back at her, formally posed and smiling in front of a man and a woman and beside a younger girl who must surely be her sister.

She stared at the photograph for a long time, and then like a faint echo a name came to mind. 'Venetia.'

As sisters they were only superficially alike. Both girls had long fair hair, but Venetia's eyes were blue, her face more square than Capri's.

Curious, she turned her attention to the adults in the picture, her eyes flicking from one to the other.

Divorced. The word entered her consciousness as she looked at the smiling couple behind the two children. They were divorced. It was like someone else saying the words inside her head, except that the voice was her own.

Opposite the family group was another photo—a classic head-and-shoulders wedding picture of herself and Rolfe. Her hair was long and piled into an elegant knot under a veil secured with a pearl coronet. Rolfe was gazing down at his bride, smiling, while Capri's eyes, her smile, were directed at the camera.

Rolfe glanced at the folder. 'Luckily that was in the zipped pocket with your passport. All I had to do was wipe a bit of water off the plastic.'

She closed it and put it back. 'Wasn't there anything else in the bag?'

'Some tissues that I threw away. A couple of sodden train and bus tickets. I couldn't find your address book, or any clue as to where you'd been staying recently. The bag was closed when I got it, but it could have fallen open at some stage. Do you know of anything that's missing?'

'No.' She had no idea what should have been in the bag, couldn't even remember owning it.

She half-dozed for much of the two-hour drive to the airport. Rolfe dropped off the hire car and hauled out an overnight bag from the back seat. Her only luggage was the plastic boutique bag.

He dug into a side pocket of his bag and produced two passports, stuffing them into the pocket of his light jacket. 'Okay,' he said, 'let's go.'

Stepping off the plane hours later at Auckland's international airport, she felt disoriented. The feeling remained as they crossed rain-wet tarseal to where Rolfe had parked his car when he'd left the country to race to her side. She was glad now of the jacket he'd bought her. Spring in New Zealand was decidedly nippy.

'Are you all right?' Rolfe asked after he'd paid the parking fee and joined the stream of traffic leaving the airport.

'Yes.' She felt as though she was in a strange land. 'How...how long have I been away?' He'd said they'd talk, but the airport bar in Sydney where they'd filled in half an hour before the flight had seemed too public, and on the plane Capri had fallen asleep again following the meal that had been served after take-off.

Rolfe braked for a traffic light. 'A couple of months,' he told her.

A long holiday. 'I can't have spent all the time on my own?' A twinge of anxiety hit her. 'Was there someone I knew on the train? Someone I was with?'

'Not that I know of,' Rolfe answered after a moment. 'There didn't seem to be anyone looking for you.'

'But...some people were killed.'

'Several, yes. I believe they were all...claimed.'

'My parents,' she said suddenly. 'Do they know—?'

'I phoned your mother in Los Angeles after the doctors told me they expected you to fully recover. She sends her love.'

'Thank you. Los Angeles? My mother's not American.'

Rolfe said carefully, 'No, she's Australian, as of course you are by birth, but she's lived in L.A. for years. So did you, for a while.'

'And Venetia?'

'Venetia too. Right now she's trying to break into films, with a bit of help from your stepfather.'

'My mother's remarried?'

'Her second husband is a photographer with contacts in the movie business.'

'What about my father? Did you contact him?'

He gave her a probing glance, then returned his attention to the road. 'I wouldn't know how to get hold of him, I'm afraid.'

Her father, then, hadn't kept in touch after the divorce. 'Why was I holidaying alone?' she asked. 'Were you too busy to come with me? You're in...' her mind fumbled for clues '...electronics or something?' Swiftly she added, 'I'm sorry. I should know, but—'

'It's okay. I own a manufacturing plant at Albany, just north of Auckland. We make laser equipment for medical and industrial use, selling to both local and international markets. It's highly specialised. I'm CEO of the firm, but the factory is run on a day-to-day basis by a very competent site manager and a team of engineers.'

'So you don't actually work there?'

'Usually I do. But I'm mainly concerned with design and development, and I have another office at home.'

'I'm...not sure where that is.'

'Atianui. A small coastal settlement an hour's drive from the factory, a bit more from Auckland.'

'Atianui.' She stumbled over the Maori syllables.

'Perhaps you'll remember it when we get there.'

She looked out of the window. Nothing out there had jelled in her memory. She blinked, lifting a hand to surreptitiously flick an unexpected tear from her cheek.

As she dropped her hand back into her lap, Rolfe's warm fingers covered hers. 'Don't worry, Capri. It will all sort itself out in the end.'

She gave a shaky sigh. His hand on hers was reassuring, strong. 'You didn't answer my question.'

'Which question was that?' Rolfe took away his hand and replaced it on the wheel. He wasn't looking at her.

'About...how I came to be holidaying in Australia on my own.'

He didn't answer immediately, speeding up to pass a couple of cars and change lanes as they approached more traffic lights. 'You decided on the spur of the moment to take this trip, and I wasn't able to get away. I can't just drop everything on a...on an impulse.'

A whim, he meant. 'But you came to the hospital.'

'Of course.'

'Have I disrupted your work?'

'Don't worry about it.'

She watched him covertly. The car moved smoothly under his guiding hands—houses, trees flashing by the windscreen. His profile was strong, like his hands, his expression remote as he concentrated on driving, only the curve of his mouth hinting at the possibility of gentleness tempering the strength and potent masculinity she'd sensed in him from the moment she'd opened her eyes and seen him standing with his back to her at the window of her hospital room. Soon they were on the Harbour Bridge, riding up the steep curve over water that sparked and flashed in the afternoon sun. She remembered this, distantly. 'The Waitemata,' she murmured, relieved that she was able to name the harbour. 'Rolfe…?'

'Yes?'

'Did we quarrel?'

It was several seconds before he answered. 'Sometimes.'

'I mean…before I left. Didn't I want you to come with me? And if you…couldn't—'

'You mean wouldn't.' He seemed to think about it. 'Let's say,' he conceded finally, 'that things were a bit strained. Never mind about that now. I'm taking you home again, and I suggest we let the past go.'

'I don't have much choice,' Capri said wryly. 'Since I don't remember it anyway.'

It was scary how few details she could recall of a whole life. Twenty-three years of it.

'You must be…' Rolfe hesitated. 'I can't imagine how you must be feeling. Confused, disoriented…

afraid?' He accelerated and changed lanes smoothly to pass a lumbering truck.

'All of the above.' She tried to sound flippant, failing abysmally.

'You're taking it remarkably well.'

'Am I? What did you expect—hysterics?'

'It wouldn't be surprising. I'm grateful you haven't resorted to that.'

'I'm not that sort of person—' She paused there, frighteningly aware that she couldn't tell what sort of person she was, and willed the wave of panic to subside. 'Am I?' she asked him.

He gave a short laugh. 'None of us sees ourselves as others do,' he said enigmatically. 'And I probably know you a lot less well than I think. While you...'

'I don't know myself at all, any more,' she said. 'That sounds very self-pitying,' she apologised, and gazed round them at the passing countryside. 'I still don't recognise any of this.'

'At least I can help there.' He described the various places they passed as if she were a tourist. When they reached the green fields and new buildings around the recently established university campus at Albany he nodded towards a side road. 'My factory is down there.'

They passed the long sweeping foreshore at Orewa, almost hidden by housing, and later the little town of Warkworth that Rolfe told her lay along a riverbank, invisible from the highway. Soon after that they turned off to take a quieter road that eventually led them to a seaside settlement of mainly new houses.

'Atianui.' Rolfe glanced at her. 'Recognise it?'

Capri shook her head. 'No.'

He swung round a corner and into a driveway, pausing momentarily to touch a button on a small black box fixed to the dashboard. Wrought-iron gates swung open and he eased the car inside the high stuccoed walls. 'It was only subdivided ten years ago—as a sort of combination dormitory town and retirement complex. We both liked the idea of living by the sea but not too far away from Auckland.'

The house was Spanish-influenced, long and low and white, with bougainvillaea, its thorny branches barely beginning to show colour, climbing the outer wall and framing an archway between the house and the two-car garage where Rolfe parked.

'I know the house.' Her relief was profound. 'I know I've seen it before.'

'Good. Of course you have.' A garage door opened and Rolfe parked and pulled on the handbrake before turning to her. 'It's your home, Capri.' He lifted a hand and gently turned her to face him, his fingers warm on her cheek. 'Welcome back, darling.'

CHAPTER THREE

His lips touched hers, sure and firm but not demanding, lingering only moments before he moved away. 'Come on,' he said. 'Let's get you inside.'

A smart little hatchback runabout occupied the other space in the garage. Rolfe said, 'That's yours. You probably shouldn't drive for a few days, though.' He took both bags from the car and put a hand on her waist to lead her to the house. Inside, she stood in a wide, terracotta-tiled hallway and looked about. 'How long have we lived here?'

'Two years,' Rolfe said matter-of-factly. 'Since we were married.'

She swallowed a dismaying desire to turn and flee. She'd been married to this man for two years, yet she knew nothing about him. Except that he was doing his best to cope with a situation that must be as difficult for him as it was for her. 'I...' She gazed around again, helplessly. 'It's not...familiar.' The disappointment was sickening. She'd been sure that once she was home everything would fall into place. But this didn't feel like home.

Rolfe touched her arm. 'I'll show you...the bedroom. Maybe you'd like to rest for a while.'

'I am tired,' she admitted. 'Although I seem to have slept a lot today.' Her skin felt stretched, her eyes heavy.

He ushered her into a spacious room overlooking the sea. The carpet was deep turquoise, the furniture white with touches of gold, the sumptuous cover on the double bed patterned in several shades of blue and green.

Most of the wall facing the ocean was tinted glass. Sliding doors opened onto a broad tiled terrace under the roof of the house, and a huge sloping archway outside the room framed the sea.

'It's a glorious view,' she said.

'Yes.' He had put down the plastic bag that she thought of as holding all her worldly possessions. 'Can I get you a drink or something? Make you a coffee?'

'No, thanks. I think I'll lie down for a while.'

'Sure.' He paused. Evidently sensing her nervous tension, he touched her cheek with his hand, the thumb rubbing gently over her skin, waking a tiny tremor of sensuous response deep within her. 'It'll be all right, Capri,' he said. 'There's nothing here to frighten you.' He dropped his hand. 'Have a good rest. I'll be around if you need anything. Just yell.'

'Thank you.' She watched him leave, still carrying his bag. He closed the door and she stood feeling lost. Hesitantly she approached the long dressing-table against one wall, touched a rather ornate gold-decorated hand-mirror lying on the white surface, and lifted a cut-glass perfume bottle, removing the stopper to sniff it. It was the same scent as the one Rolfe had bought her before they left Australia. Spicy, faintly earthy—a very sexy perfume. 'Your favourite,' he'd said.

Turning, she opened a door and found a walk-in wardrobe filled with clothes. She touched some of the garments, moved them along on their hangers. They were all her size, colours that suited her. Most of them looked expensive. Easily thirty pairs of shoes sat neatly in pairs along the floor. It seemed an awful lot.

Fingering a peacock-blue silk dress, she frowned.

Rolfe was presumably quite well-off. He had a thriving business, and this house in its exclusive coastal enclave was certainly not cheap real estate.

Perhaps she had come from more modest circumstances? Where had they met? She must ask him later.

Nothing here had triggered her elusive memory, and her shoulders drooped as she left the wardrobe and opened another door into a white and turquoise bathroom.

Here too the floor was carpeted. There was a roomy glass-fronted shower, a marble bathtub almost big enough for two, and all the taps were large and gold-plated.

Seeing another door on the opposite side of the bathroom, she tapped on the panels and opened it on a bedroom identical to the one she'd come from, right down to the bedspread, on which Rolfe's overnight bag sat.

She closed the door quickly, her emotions a mixture of shame and relief. Was he going to sleep there?

Rolfe was her husband and she'd been away for two months. Instinctively she knew that he was a man who appreciated sex—his virility was so much a part of his personality she couldn't be unaware of it. The way he looked at her and touched her made her conscious of her femininity, and even that brief welcome-home kiss in the garage had held a hint of sexuality, of passion.

But although she'd reacted blindly to his masculine attraction since she'd woken to see him waiting for her return to consciousness, what she had told him in the hospital was the truth. So far as she was concerned he might have been a total stranger. And she wasn't a woman who would—or could—make love with a man she scarcely knew.

How could she *know* that with such certainty? she

wondered, stripping the cover from the bed in the room that was evidently to be hers.

Moving slowly, she removed her shoes and lay down, glad to have her head rest on cool, clean linen. She supposed that although her mind for some reason refused to remember events, places or people, deep down she was still the same Capri she'd always been. Personality remained, even when memory was absent. Her essential self hadn't altered. It was a comforting thought.

She woke to gathering darkness, the room dimmed and the sea outside grey and sleek with gold highlights.

Momentarily disoriented, she sat up and pushed back her hair. The room, the view were alien to her. Remnants of a dream clung. Familiar voices, a house with tall pale trees around it...

Then she remembered the hospital, Rolfe, the journey home, and the wardrobe full of expensive clothing.

She swung her feet to the thick carpeting and crossed to the dressing-table.

There were three drawers along the top, all holding a variety of makeup and grooming products—bottles, jars, mascara wands. She found a comb and closed the drawer, deciding she needed a shower.

In the bathroom a brass shelf held a stack of thick, clean towels above a heated rail. She hung her clothes from a brass hook and stepped into the shower.

Recessed shelves held scented soap and bottles of shampoo and matching conditioners. The water was hot and forceful. She let it run over her for several minutes, shampooed her hair, and closed her eyes to allow the spray to rinse out the foam.

A sound made her turn her head, and through the

steam she saw Rolfe standing in the doorway from her bedroom.

Her immediate reaction was to raise one hand across her breasts and lower the other in the Venus pose.

'Are you all right?' Rolfe demanded.

'Yes. Thank you.'

He nodded and withdrew, closing the door.

Stupid, stupid, she chided herself, turning off the water. She grabbed a towel and rubbed at her hair, then quickly took another, dried her body and wrapped the towel about it, tucking the ends firmly under her arms.

When she entered the bedroom Rolfe was standing at the window, reminding her of the first time she had seen him.

No, not the first time, she corrected herself. The first time she *remembered* seeing him...

He glanced over his shoulder at her, and then reached to draw the curtains across the window. 'People walk along the beach.' He turned to face her. 'Now and then one of them will climb the bank. You don't want to entertain peeping Toms.' The room seemed smaller now, more intimate. 'I'm sorry if I embarrassed you.' His slight smile was crooked. 'I'm afraid I didn't think...and I was a bit worried. You're only just out of hospital—'

'It's all right,' she said. 'It was...silly of me to be so—'

'Shy?' he suggested as she groped for the right word. 'It certainly didn't seem like you, Capri.' His gaze slid over her, making her conscious of her nakedness under the towel.

She felt her body flush. 'I...suppose I'd got over any shyness with you, after being married for two years.'

'Oh, I think quite a while before that.'

'Does that mean we...?' She paused. 'I mean, were we...lovers for a long time before we got married?'

'Several months.' His eyes glittered and narrowed, as if her thoughtless query had evoked some erotic memory. 'You'd better get dressed. You'll be cold.'

It wasn't in the least cold—the house was surprisingly warm—but she turned to the wardrobe she'd discovered earlier, then hesitated. 'What should I wear? Are we...do you have any plans for this evening?'

'Don't tempt me.' Again that disconcerting flare of sexual awareness lit Rolfe's eyes, and she put a hand on the edge of the towel that covered her breasts, nervously checking it was secure.

His voice changed and became crisp. 'Wear whatever you're comfortable in. I assumed you wouldn't feel like eating out tonight, so I got a few supplies in while you were asleep.'

If he knew she'd slept, then he'd looked in on her before. How long had he watched her while she was oblivious?

Mentally she shook herself. He'd been concerned. 'Do you want me to cook?' she asked him.

'Good lord, no! I can rustle up some kind of meal.'

She couldn't stand around wearing nothing but a towel. Turning to the walk-in wardrobe again, she murmured, 'Excuse me,' went in and half shut the door.

When she had dressed and come out again Rolfe had gone. About to close the door of the wardrobe, she paused, surveying herself in the mirror on the back of it. The loose cream silk shirt and dark green trousers suited her colouring and they fitted perfectly. Yet she felt as though she was wearing someone else's clothes.

Her hair was still damp. She went into the bathroom and hunted in the drawers under the vanity unit, coming up with, as she'd half expected, a hand-dryer. There was a safety plug near the basin, and in ten minutes her hair was dry—silky soft and bouncy with the underlying wave that had always created problems.

Always? For a moment memory seemed almost within her grasp. And then there was nothing.

She brushed the style into shape, then padded back to the wardrobe and, after a brief indecision, slipped her feet into bronze pumps, one of the few pairs of shoes that didn't have high heels. Then she opened the door and ventured into the turquoise-carpeted passageway.

The aroma of frying meat led her to the kitchen, a spacious room that gleamed with stainless steel and whiteware. Rolfe turned from the stove top set into one of the wide counters. He smiled, his eyes studying her thoroughly and making her skin prickle, not unpleasantly.

'Can I do anything?' she asked.

'Finish off the salad if you like.' He indicated a glass bowl half filled with lettuce leaves. 'You'll find tomatoes and cucumber in the fridge.' Turning back to the stove top, he took a pair of stainless-steel tongs from a wall rack to flip the chops over.

Looking about, she found the refrigerator, first opening the door of the matching freezer by mistake.

She placed the vegetables on the bench and rummaged in a drawer for a few seconds before Rolfe looked around and asked, 'What do you want?'

'A knife?'

He directed her to the wooden block by the refrigerator where she found several knives of different sizes. By the time she'd finished the salad, Rolfe was turning down the heat under the chops. A beeping noise made her look at the microwave oven at one end of the workbench.

'Can you turn those spuds?' Rolfe asked her.

She opened the door and dealt with the two potatoes in their jackets, then restarted the machine.

When she turned away again Rolfe was watching her with a curious stare.

'What is it?' she said.

'You seem to be familiar with the microwave.'

She hadn't thought about it. 'Yes,' she agreed, momentarily pleased. Perhaps if she just let things happen without thinking too much, skills and memories would return to her. 'I must have used it before.'

'Frequently.' He gave her a slightly taut grin. 'As soon as the potatoes are done we can eat.'

Rolfe carried their plates to an adjoining dining room while she brought along the cutlery they needed. He'd already flung a cloth over the small table that fitted into a half-circle of windows. A longer table flanked by high-backed chairs occupied most of the remaining floor space.

The curtains were open, and moths and insects flung themselves against the dark glass. A particularly loud thump made Capri glance up from cutting into her baked potato, and she gasped at the huge brown winged beetle, long feelers waving madly, trying to gain access through the window.

'It's only a huhu.' Rolfe got up to jerk the curtains closed over the window, then sat down again.

The beetle hurled itself twice more at the window, and then apparently gave up and flew away. Relieved, she said, 'The insects here are pretty rampant.'

'Only at night. How's your chop?'

'Fine. You're a good cook.'

'I have a few basic skills.'

'I'll do the cooking tomorrow.'

He looked up, a fork poised in his hand, then nodded. 'If you feel up to it.'

She helped him clear the table, and watched as he placed the dishes in a machine. 'It hardly seems worth it,' she commented, 'for just a few dishes.'

He straightened, closing the lid, and his brows lifted slightly. 'You've always had a firm belief that labour-saving devices are there to be used.'

'Well...I suppose...' She shrugged. There was some sense in that.

For a moment she had a weird sensation of being lost in a dark, unknown place, blindly groping for something to cling to.

'Capri?' Rolfe's hand was on her shoulder, his eyes probing hers. 'What is it?'

'I just...I don't know. For a minute I...didn't know where I was.'

He grasped both her shoulders, but not hard. 'You're home, Capri,' he said. 'It's all right.'

Something snapped. 'It's not all right!' she retorted sharply. 'I feel like an intruder in my own bedroom, my own wardrobe, I don't know my way around, and I can't even remember where the damned knives are kept!'

He gave a small, not unsympathetic laugh, but in her oversensitive state even that stung.

Her voice notched a note higher. 'It's not a joke! And how do I know you're really my husband? I've no recollection of being married to you!'

And that, she realised, remembering the wedding photograph in her bag, was a pretty stupid thing to say.

The smile had disappeared from Rolfe's mouth. 'Believe me, I don't think it's at all funny, Capri. But I am your husband, and you're my wife!'

The air had thickened between them, and everything seemed to go still. She was overwhelmingly conscious of his strength, his nearness, his masculinity, and her breath caught in her throat, a tiny pulse hammering at its base.

He drew in a breath too, and she remembered that moment in the hospital when he'd seemed to be affected by the scent of her, and she'd seen his nostrils dilate and his eyes darken as they did now.

His hands slipped from her shoulders to the bare skin of her arms. His expression went taut and purposeful. 'Maybe this will help,' he said, and pulled her closer, his arms sliding about her as her head involuntarily tipped back, and then he caught her mouth under the warm impact of his.

The kiss was intimate and insistent, the warmth and hardness of his body pressing against hers, unfamiliar and a little frightening, even though her blood sang and her lips involuntarily parted under his persuasion. His hold was firm but deliberately gentle, as if he had remembered that her bruises were still tender.

Now her head was cradled against his arm, and his mouth demanded a response that she gave at first tentatively and then with increasing passion, until he shifted their positions and manoeuvred her up against the work-bench, and with his strong hands under her arms lifted her and sat her on the counter, his mouth freeing hers and his hands going to the buttons of her blouse.

But the mindless spell had broken. 'No!' Her fingers closed frantically over his, stopping him.

'No?' His voice was hoarse, and he spread his hands under the feeble constraint of hers, big palms cupping her breasts through the flimsy fabric. Then his expression tightened. 'Did I hurt you?'

'You didn't hurt me, but—don't, Rolfe! I'm not ready for this.'

'Damn it, Capri—'

She gripped his wrists, her cheeks hot and her body trembling. 'Please—'

His hands moved to her face, his eyes subjecting her to a hard, furious inspection. 'Are you saying you don't want me?'

'I'm saying I don't want...this.' She still held his wrists. 'I know you have every right, but—'

'*Right?*' He dropped his hands then and stepped back. 'The time is long past when a man could claim his *right* to his wife's body, Capri. Do you think I'd force my way into your bed?'

'No! No, I don't think that.' Her hands clenched on the counter on either side of her. 'But...please try to understand. I'm not...comfortable about going to bed with someone I...feel I hardly know.'

Rolfe gave a short, disbelieving laugh. 'Really?' It was obvious she'd thrown him off balance, his rigid control cracking. His eyes were hard and brilliant as onyx. 'It didn't stop you before!'

CHAPTER FOUR

'WHAT?' She felt her eyes dilate painfully, her throat lock.

A spasm seemed to cross Rolfe's face. He lifted a hand and thrust back a stubborn strand of dark hair that had strayed to his forehead. 'Never mind.'

'I do mind! What did you mean?'

'Just that you were in my bed within hours of our first meeting. So excuse me if I find it a bit ironic that you're being so coy about making love to me now.'

She stared at him in disbelief. *'Hours?'* She couldn't comprehend this. It sounded so...wrong.

'Lust at first sight.' He grinned narrowly. Then he must have noticed her instinctive recoil. 'I'm sorry if the word offends you, but one could hardly call it love...'

'What happened?' They'd taken one look at each other and fallen into bed? He was a very attractive, sexy man and she could well believe she'd have been tempted, but it seemed so out of character...

Again her lack of real knowledge taunted her. What did she know about her own character, how she might have reacted, what sort of lifestyle she'd led before marrying Rolfe?

'What happened?' Rolfe repeated. 'We met at a party in L.A. You were with someone, I was alone. You were...' his eyes glazed slightly as though he was looking at a distant memory '...stunning.'

Her lips parted, her heart thudding disconcertingly. In some level of her subconscious she was aware this wasn't the first time she'd been complimented on her looks. Only surely never with the intensity that she heard now in Rolfe's voice.

His eyes refocused, studying her, and the intensity changed to self-mockery. 'It was like all the romantic movies you've ever seen. We looked at each other across a crowded room and from that moment there was no one else there for either of us. You smiled, I walked over and introduced myself. I tried to be civilised, talk to the man you were with, other people. I have no idea what I said to them. We danced. Your date...' He paused, a faintly regretful expression darkening his eyes. 'Your date got drunk and aggressive, and I offered you a lift home. In the car I asked if you'd like to come to my hotel for a nightcap, and you looked straight into my eyes and said yes, that would be nice.' Again he paused. 'We hadn't even kissed. But when we got to the hotel I gave you the choice of having a drink in the public bar or raiding the minibar in my suite. You chose the suite.' He smiled crookedly, reminiscently, his eyes gleaming under hooded lids as he looked at her. 'We never did have that nightcap.'

She was staring at him. He shoved his hands into his pockets. 'You don't remember any of this?'

Silently she shook her head. He might have been describing some other woman entirely. A woman who was sexually confident to the point of recklessness, willing to take incredible chances with an exciting stranger. 'Had I been drinking?'

His brows rose. 'It was a party. But you weren't drunk. I wouldn't take advantage of a tipsy woman, Capri.'

But maybe she'd had enough alcohol to affect her judgement, to topple her inhibitions and send her into a stranger's arms. A stranger who had attracted her so strongly that she'd boldly beckoned him with a smile, had neglected the man who'd accompanied her to the party, and gone home with the interloper. Not only gone home with him, but slept with him that same night. She had no reason to doubt Rolfe's account of their meeting, and she could believe that she'd been fascinated by his striking looks, his confident sexuality, and his overt interest, but at the same time she was convinced that the behaviour he described wasn't normal for her.

Rolfe moved towards her, his hands going to her waist. He studied her face, his eyes very dark and enigmatic. Then he tightened his grip and lifted her down, and she felt his lips brush her forehead before he let her go. 'Maybe we were in too much of a hurry back then. This could give us another chance.'

'Another chance?'

'To get to know each other again,' he suggested. 'It'll be…different this time.'

'I want to get to know you,' she told him, still feeling breathless. 'Thank you for being so understanding.'

His continued scrutiny of her turned curious, even puzzled. He nodded. 'It could be…my pleasure,' he said rather obscurely.

She looked away from the disturbing light in his eyes. 'Do you mind if I wander around—familiarise myself with the house?'

'It's your home, Capri. Would you like me to come with you?'

'In case I get lost?' She gave him a pale smile. It was a big house, but hardly a castle.

'In case you want to ask questions.' His eyes cooling, he asked abruptly, 'You're not faking this, are you?'

She blinked. *'Faking?'*

Impatiently, Rolfe shook his head. 'No, of course not,' he answered himself. 'There's no reason—'

'Well, you'd know better than me about that!' she said with a spurt of indignation. 'Why would *anyone* want to fake amnesia? It's no picnic!'

'It was just a thought.'

'You have very strange thoughts!'

'You don't know the half of them.' His eyes held hers, sending hot shivers down her spine. He moved away from her. 'Go and take your tour of the house,' he said. 'I'll be in the lounge if you want me. You do know where that is?'

'Yes, we passed it on the way in.'

She left it until last, after she had seen the several bedrooms and another bathroom, the utility room, and one that must be Rolfe's office, with bookshelves, filing cabinets and a desktop computer. And a room that held a sewing machine, a work-table strewn with paper templates, and shelves filled with pattern books, fashion magazines, and piles of fabric, a sumptuous collection of colour and texture. A dressmaker's adjustable form stood in one corner, and here too there was a computer, with a box of disks beside it.

She retraced her steps to the wide lobby-cum-passageway and the double doors leading to the lounge. Like the rest of the house, the large room was furnished with taste and discernment—she could almost picture the words in some glossy magazine.

Rolfe was sprawled on a long off-white sofa, reading a newspaper and listening to something she vaguely thought was Mozart. She said, 'I found the sewing room.'

'Yes?' He swung his feet onto the carpet and picked

up a remote control, muting the music to a low background sound.

'Am I a dressmaker?'

Rolfe smiled with a hint of incredulity. 'A dressmaker? You'd hate to be called that. Come over here.' He indicated the space on the sofa beside him and folded the paper, putting it aside on an elegant glass table.

Tensely she walked over and sat down, leaving two feet of space between them. 'It doesn't look like a home sewing room,' she said. 'It's a workroom. What did I do?'

'You do some fashion design,' he said patiently. 'You're quite talented. Although...'

'Although what?'

He shrugged. 'You've come close to winning awards a couple of times, but...your temperament isn't suited to steady work. You have flashes of inspiration, work on them like mad for a few weeks, and need as many weeks to recover—and, I suppose, to allow the creative juices to flow again. It isn't a style that adjusts well to the business world.'

Digesting that, she glanced around the room. The long sofas arranged in a U-shape with glass end tables, and the group of chairs around another, larger glass table looked comfortable enough. The pictures on the walls were originals and she recognised the signatures on a couple of them.

The drapes that Rolfe had drawn against the night were textured faille silk, well chosen to complement the turquoise carpet used throughout the house, and in the daytime to frame the view of the sea and echo its colours.

Everything was beautifully co-ordinated and money had not been stinted. But she felt like a visitor here.

'Who decorated the rooms?' she asked. 'And who designed the house?'

'One of Auckland's top architects did the house. And we hired an interior designer. You wanted perfection and insisted on expert advice. What's the matter?'

She had shifted restlessly, oddly dissatisfied. 'Nothing. It's a lovely room.'

It *was* a lovely room, only it seemed to lack warmth. She supposed that in summer the cool effect might be an asset.

The music had stopped. 'Was that Mozart?' she asked.

'Yes—I know you'd prefer something a bit livelier. The tapes and discs are over there under the player. Why don't you choose one?'

Hesitantly she got up and went over to the built-in unit holding the music centre, knelt and opened the top drawer.

Rolfe said, 'Most of yours are in the second drawer down.'

She opened the next drawer. The first few labels meant little, but then she found a CD that she lifted out with delight—an album by a New Zealand group that had made the pop charts both in their home country and overseas. 'This is one of my favourites!'

'Yes.' Rolfe had approached silently across the carpet and was standing just behind her, looking over her shoulder. 'You used to play it a lot.'

And her subconscious had remembered. 'Can we play it now?' She twisted to look up at him.

'Feel free.'

She turned back to the music centre, inspecting the rows of buttons and dials. It took her a minute to locate the CD component. 'Here?' she asked, checking.

'Right.'

She slid out the disc that was already there and replaced it with the new one. Nothing happened, and Rolfe said, 'You need to press the "play" button.'

Her fingers hovered as she read the labels on the various buttons, then touched one. 'This?'

'Yes.'

The music began, barely audible, and she asked, 'Where's the volume control?'

'Here.' His lean fingers turned the knob. A hand briefly lighted on her shoulder, then he offered it to help her up.

Taking it, she rose to her feet. 'Thank you. Don't you like pop music?'

'Some.' He let go her hand. 'These guys are musicians. They know what they're doing.'

'So we have tastes in common.'

He regarded her strangely. 'I guess we do.'

Her lips parted, her tongue caught for a moment between her teeth. 'Of course we do, or we'd never have married.'

His laugh was brief. 'That's a remarkably naive view of marriage, for you.'

'For me?'

'For anyone,' he amended swiftly. 'Don't they say opposites attract?'

'Do they? I mean, yes, I know people say that but...I'm not sure it's a good basis for marriage. *Are* we opposites?'

'Some people might have thought so,' he allowed. 'But we were both willing to take a gamble on our relationship. Perhaps for different reasons.'

'Different reasons? What were they?'

He was silent, staring down at her. 'I can't speak for you,' he said. 'It wouldn't be fair. And as for myself...'

Shrugging, he turned away to go back to the sofa. 'I suppose I was in love.'

'You suppose?' Following him, she stopped short as he sat down, facing her.

When he looked up his eyes had a strange, glazed glitter in them. His smile twisted. 'All right,' he said, and reached forward, his hand closing about her wrist to tug her down beside him.

He retained his hold, looking at the hand he held, his thumb stroking over the back of it. 'I don't know what else to call it.' His voice was low and strained.

He'd called it lust earlier, she remembered. Lust at first sight, he'd said, describing their meeting.

'It's not my habit,' he told her, 'to take a woman I've just met to bed—no matter how willing she is. For months I could hardly see straight for wanting you. You were...an obsession.'

'And you resented it.' She stated the fact baldly.

He seemed startled, his eyes meeting hers, searching her face. 'Maybe I did in a way. I wasn't used to that level of...distraction.'

'Distraction?'

'I have a demanding, complex business to run. Ever since I left university I've been building it, expanding it. There wasn't time for much else in my life. Or energy. And then suddenly there was you. For a time I felt as if I'd lost control.'

'You'd hate that.' She knew as surely as if he'd spelled it out for her that Rolfe liked being in control of himself, of his life.

And of his wife? The wayward thought made her shiver inside. Just how *had* he felt, how had he reacted, when she'd insisted on visiting Australia without him? She'd sensed anger in him several times since she'd woken in that hospital room—anger controlled and usually well concealed, but simmering beneath the surface.

Rolfe released her hand and sighed, settling into the corner of the sofa, one arm laid along the back. 'Hate it?' he repeated. 'The most exciting sex I'd had in my entire life?'

'Sex?' Capri clamped her hands together. 'You just said you fell in love.'

'Sometimes it's hard to separate the two. Harder, they say, for men than women. Perhaps that's true.'

'Perhaps,' she agreed tentatively. 'I don't think I would have found it so difficult.'

'Don't you?' He regarded her pensively.

Her gaze slid aside. Maybe she was wrong. At this moment she was fighting a strong urge to close the small space between them and rest her head against his chest, feel his arms about her. Could that be love? Perhaps her body, her heart, remembered what her mind refused to give up to consciousness.

'Listen.' He tipped his head back, angling it to concentrate on the music from the hidden speakers. Two voices blended against a subtle, haunting melody.

> Burning like a rocket
> exploding into stars
> most splendid in its dying
> is this love of ours

The song was called 'Fire in the Sky'. She loved the tune, but the words saddened her, telling of a love that had flared briefly, incandescently.

> too bright to last the distance
> a fire in the sky.

'He knows,' Rolfe murmured.

'He?'

'The guy who wrote the song.' He turned his head, his eyes half closed and gleaming, his mouth cynical. 'Doesn't he?'

'It isn't like that with me!'

Rolfe's attitude was relaxed but very still. Something stirred in those almost-hidden dark eyes. 'How would you know?' he enquired softly.

'I know if I really loved someone it would be for ever. Not some flash in the pan, like in the song.'

'You sound as though you mean it.'

'I just *know* that's how it is, for me.'

'Really.' Although he still hadn't shifted his position, his hand was tightly gripping the back of the sofa. 'And yet you left me.'

'Left you?' She stared at him.

Rolfe stirred then, sitting up but not meeting her eyes. 'To go off to Australia without me.'

'But that was a holiday...wasn't it?' Doubt sneaked in and a hollow feeling opened in her stomach. 'Do you mean I didn't intend to come back? But...if we were separated, I'm here under false pretences—' The thought was frightening. If their marriage had ended, if he didn't really want her here, she had no right to be with him, and where could she go? A sliver of fear chilled her.

'We weren't separated,' he said quickly. 'I refused to drop everything and go to Australia at a moment's notice, that's all. We...argued over it.'

'So I went anyway. But I wouldn't have walked out on you over that—would I?'

Rolfe studied her quietly. 'No, of course you

wouldn't. But you see, you left no word.'

It was a calm, unemotional condemnation. She'd gone with no explanation, no promise to return? That was more than thoughtless. Even if they had quarrelled, it was cruel. Surely more so than he'd deserved.

She swallowed, and her voice, when she finally spoke through her shock and shame, was husky. 'Were you very angry?'

His hand released the sofa-back as he spread the fingers, palm upwards. 'Does it matter? It's all in the past. We both probably said things we shouldn't have, and you wanted to punish me. There's no point in going over it all now.'

Another song had begun, and Rolfe turned away from her, listening to the music. His eyelids lowered, and she thought he must be tired. Flying across the Tasman, keeping watch at her bedside, then organising the flight home with her and driving here from the airport would have exhausted most people. He hadn't rested this afternoon as she had. Possibly he had even spent some hours catching up on work that must have been abandoned when he made the unscheduled journey.

She had lots more questions but they could wait. Trying to relax, she sat back against the cushions and listened.

When the disc had finished Rolfe got up and removed it. 'Want to play another?' he asked her.

'I think I'll go to bed. I know I've already had a rest, but...' It seemed to have been a tiring day, with the flight from one country to another, and the emotional stress.

'Fine.' She wondered if he was relieved. 'Do you have all that you need?'

'I'm sure I'll find everything. Goodnight, Rolfe.'

He came over to her and lifted her face with a hand under her chin. His eyes searched hers as though asking permission, and then he bent and brushed a kiss across her cheek. 'Sleep well,' he said.

In the bedroom she opened drawers and found satin and lace bras, sexy panties, slinky slips in several colours, heavily edged with lace, and a dozen or more nightgowns, some short and sassy, some long and glamorous, several folded under matching semi-transparent wraps frothed with lace.

Had she ever worn these enticing, blatantly sexy gowns? She supposed she had.

She shook out the plainest she could find, a deep red satin gown with shoestring straps, a cross over bodice, and a skirt that hugged her hips and brushed her ankles and was slit high in front.

The satin slipped over her skin when she drew the garment on, and she caught a glimpse of herself in the dressing-table mirror as she bent to close the drawer, the low-cut bodice exposing the full curves of her breasts. She straightened, staring at her reflection, and had a momentary fantasy of Rolfe standing behind her, sliding his arms about her, pulling her back against him.

Shaking her head impatiently, she backed away and was about to get into the big double bed when a thought hit her.

Returning to the drawers, she opened all of them one by one, rummaged among the laces and satins and the stored woollens and T-shirts and several pairs of track pants. Then she went to the wardrobe for a riffle through the hangers, confirming she'd missed nothing in there.

Back in the bedroom, she stood wrapped in thought

before slowly climbing into bed. Rolfe had made it clear he didn't intend to join her there tonight, and she'd been grateful for his consideration, his sensitivity.

But he had not had time to remove everything of his from a room they had previously shared. No way.

Yet there wasn't one vestige of evidence that he had ever used this room as his own. No clothing, no masculine toiletries, not so much as a comb. Nothing. Every personal possession here was overtly, overwhelmingly, feminine.

So for how long had she and Rolfe, her husband, had separate rooms?

CHAPTER FIVE

IT WAS fully daylight when Capri woke. In the bathroom there was a lingering warmth and dampness. Rolfe must have used the shower not long ago.

She pulled on jeans and a shirt over a bra and pants from one of the drawers she'd rifled through last night. Rolfe was in the kitchen, a half cup of coffee and a crumb-dusted plate before him. When she entered he put down the folded newspaper in his hand. 'Good morning. How are you feeling?'

'I feel fine.' Her head no longer hurt and her bruises were already fading. 'How did you sleep?'

His eyes flickered. 'All right.' He stood up and pulled out another chair. 'Can I get you some toast—coffee?'

'Thanks, I can manage. Why don't you sit down?'

She found the bread on the counter near the toaster and dropped in two slices.

'I've finished anyway.' He drained his cup, put it together with his plate, and carried them to the dishwasher. 'I need to go to the factory today. Will you be all right? Hallie will be in later—the cleaner.'

'We have a cleaner?'

'Twice a week. It's a big house. Do you want me to stay until she arrives?'

She could see he was anxious to go but unsure about leaving her. 'It's all right. I can explain.'

He looked at her thoughtfully. 'No,' he said with sudden decision, 'I'm not sure you should be alone yet. I'll just make a couple of phone calls and let people know to expect me a bit later.'

By the time he'd done that and come back to the kitchen, she'd finished her toast and coffee.

She offered him another cup, but he shook his head, instead prowling restlessly as she put her dishes in the machine and wiped up crumbs from the bench.

'Hallie will do that,' he told her.

'I suppose so, but I was taught to clean up after myself.' How had she known that?

Rolfe looked at her with a surprised grin. 'That's the first I've heard of it.'

'Well...most of us don't always live up to what our mothers taught us.' Reminded, she added, 'Shouldn't I phone her, by the way—my mother? What's the time in Los Angeles?'

'Too early. Wait a few hours and then you won't be getting her out of bed.'

'You said you didn't know where my father was. Would my mother know?'

'I doubt it. I gather she wanted nothing more to do with him after the divorce.' He gave her one of his searching looks. 'You haven't remembered any more?'

'No. I remembered my sister and my parents when I saw their picture. Maybe if I looked at some more photographs—are there some about?'

'There are albums on the bookshelves in the living room.'

'I'll get them out later.' She crossed to the sink to rinse out the cloth she'd used to wipe up the toast crumbs. Her eye was caught by the bougainvillaea on the wall that divided the section from the road. Although it was only just unfurling its leaves, in her mind she could clearly see it in all its summer splendour, smothered in purple. 'It's a lovely garden.' The hibiscus were already bearing a few open scarlet blooms, and a brilliant orange-flaming tropical rhododendron flamed against the white wall. 'Did we plant it ourselves? Who looks after it?'

'We got a landscape designer in, and his staff did the planting. And we have a guy who mows the lawn every week and trims shrubs when they need it. It's low-maintenance—no flowerbeds, just shrubs.'

The black wrought-iron gate in the white wall opened, and a plump, dark-haired young woman entered.

'Is that Hallie?' Capri asked.

'Yes, her name's Hallie Switzer.'

He opened the door himself, and the young woman came in. 'Morning, Mr Massey. Mrs Massey—you're home! I heard you were in that terrible train crash in Aussie. Are you all right?'

Rolfe answered for her. 'My wife had concussion and it's temporarily affected her memory, Hallie, so don't be surprised if she doesn't remember things she would have known before.'

Hallie looked at Capri with curiosity. 'That's rough—I'm really sorry.'

'I have to go now,' Rolfe said, 'but call me, Hallie, if you have any reason to be concerned. She only came out of hospital yesterday.'

'Sure thing. You take it easy, Mrs Massey. I'll try not to disturb you.'

'I've left some money on my desk for you,' Rolfe told the woman. 'I hope to be back early this afternoon,' he added to Capri. 'So you won't be on your own for long after Hallie's finished. Don't leave the house, will you?'

'Rolfe, the doctors wouldn't have let me come home if—'

'Please,' he said. 'Humour me, okay? I'll phone to check after Hallie's gone, make sure you're okay.' His hand cupped her cheek while he gave her a brief kiss.

When he'd left she wandered into the living room while Hallie busied herself in the kitchen.

A framed photograph stood among the books and the few well-placed ceramic art pieces on a set of shelves above the entertainment centre—the same wedding picture of Capri and Rolfe that had been in the folder in her bag. She studied it, then hunted out the photograph albums he'd spoken of.

There were childhood pictures of her with and without her sister, a few photos of her parents, and many of herself as she grew older, with groups of boys and girls, others with a succession of young men.

A second album was filled with photos of her and Rolfe's wedding. There seemed to have been a lot of people there, including her mother, and her sister Venetia as one of four bridesmaids. Venetia looked older but otherwise not much different from the photo in Capri's bag.

Although she pored over every face none gave her any feeling that she'd ever known them.

A third album held cuttings from magazines as well as photographic prints. Glamour shots on glossy paper.

Her own face smiled, pouted, looked provocatively over her shoulder or haughtily into the camera. She'd been a photographic model. Her hair was long and silky-looking, and in many of the photos her eyes looked bigger, her cheeks thinner, her mouth fuller, but there was no denying the face was hers. She guessed that makeup and photographic techniques accounted for the difference.

Some of the captions had her name in them—Capri

Rivera. Was it really her maiden name, or perhaps one that she'd only used professionally? There was no sense of connection, no faint echo of recall. A few photographs showed other women modelling clothes 'designed by Capri Rivera'. That should make her proud. But she felt totally detached.

Dispirited, she put aside the books and got up, wandering to the window. The hum of a vacuum cleaner came from somewhere in the house. She sighed, then turned decisively and walked along the passageway to the room where surely she had spent a lot of time.

The sewing machine and computer must have been tools that she was accustomed to using. She touched the computer with its blank screen, found the 'on' switch and flicked it. The machine hummed and the screen lit up, showing a menu of choices. One item was 'Designmate' and she hesitated, then moved the cursor to it and pressed 'Enter' before sliding into the typist's chair in front of her.

When the program opened she stared at the options presented. Experimenting, she gleaned some idea of what the program was supposed to do—provide alternative views of fashion design elements, and help the user produce templates for garments. But her fumbling efforts were those of a total novice.

She switched off the computer, sitting for a few minutes with her head in her hands before she straightened her shoulders and got up.

Hallie was in the passageway, a spray can of furniture polish in one hand, a dust-cloth in the other.

'Can I help with something?' Capri asked. 'Where were you headed with those?'

'I was going to do Mr Massey's office.'

'Let me.'

She held out her hand and Hallie gave her the cleaning things, saying doubtfully, 'Are you sure, Mrs Massey?'

'I'm sure. Hallie—how long have you been working for us?'

'About a year.'

'Don't you think you could call me Capri?'

Hallie's eyes widened. She opened her mouth, then seemed to think better of what she'd been going to say. 'If you like,' she said finally.

'Thanks.' With a grateful smile, Capri moved off.

Aware that her insistence on doing Rolfe's room was an excuse, she dusted shelves, wiped the wide window-ledge, and straightened the piled papers on the big desk where the computer stood, glancing at letterheads as she dusted behind a tiered paper tray.

There was nothing here to indicate the personality of the occupant except the ordered appearance of the room. Rolfe could surely lay his hands instantly on whatever file or document he needed.

She had no watch, but an electronic clock on the desk told her it was nearly eleven. Rolfe had said that in a 'few hours' she could telephone her mother.

Opening drawers, she found various pens, trays of paper clips and boxes of computer disks, an Auckland area telephone book, but no address book, no list of telephone numbers.

A large framed photograph lay face down among the envelopes and pens in a lower drawer.

She picked it up, turning it to find her own face smiling through the glass. Her hair was long, tumbling onto bare shoulders, and one strap of the low-cut dress she wore had slipped down her arm. Her lips were glossily reddened and her eyes bright and inviting.

Hallie appeared in the doorway, a vacuum cleaner hose in her hand. 'Shall I come back later?'

Capri returned the photograph to the drawer and closed it. 'I've finished in here.'

There was a phone in the big entrance lobby, on a table with a drawer underneath that yielded a second directory with a few names and numbers scribbled in the back pages. None seemed to be preceded by an American prefix. Nor were any of the names familiar. She realised she didn't even know what name to look for if it wasn't under M for mother...

In her bedroom where yet another telephone stood on the night table there was a small leather-bound book beside it, but the alphabetical entries meant nothing to her.

Hallie left at twelve-thirty, and fifteen minutes later the phone rang. Capri answered it in the hallway.

'Are you all right?' Rolfe's voice queried. 'Has Hallie gone?'

'Yes, and I'm fine.'

Before she had time to ask for her mother's phone number he was speaking again, sounding hurried. 'I'll be home in a couple of hours. Can you manage on your own until then?'

'I'm not crippled or anything, Rolfe.'

There was a pause and she imagined him frowning into space, drumming his fingers on a big desk like the one in his office here. 'I'll be there as soon as I can,' he promised. 'Have you had lunch?'

'No, but I'll get myself something.'

'Do. I'll see you later.'

She was asleep on one of the couches in the big living room when he arrived. Sensing his presence, she opened her eyes to find him standing over her.

He said, 'I disturbed you.' And then, as if the huskily spoken words were wrung from him, 'You're very lovely, Capri.'

She started to sit up, wondering how long he'd been there. 'I didn't mean to fall asleep. I was reading.' The glossy magazine had fallen to the carpet.

He dropped to the sofa beside her, preventing her from bringing her feet to the floor. One lean hand brushed a strand of hair back from her cheek to tuck it behind her ear. 'Stay there,' he said.

'But I...'

'Shh.' His hand slipped behind her head, and he bent towards her, his lips barely meeting hers, warm and un- demanding as they brushed across hers, a fleeting touch repeated once, twice, before he drew back a couple of inches. 'Do you mind?'

'No.' Her answer was a breath, a whisper.

He smiled, then brought his mouth back to hers, this time covering it with his own, exerting the faintest pres- sure until her lips parted, but not taking advantage of that, keeping the kiss just on the edge of passion, defi- nitely sexual but restrained and gently questing.

Trustingly, she followed his lead, giving in to the gradual seduction of his mouth, letting him deepen the kiss to a hungry seeking, until he broke away, his hand still curved about her nape, and stared down at her, his eyes hot and very dark.

She stared numbly back, hectic colour burning her cheeks, her body alight. She realised she was clinging to his sleeve, and drew her hand away.

His eyes narrowed and he angled his head question- ingly. 'You don't want to take this further?'

Her tongue moistened her lower lip. It was disturbing, this depth of desire. She wasn't even sure what she was so wary of, but knew instinctively that she ran the risk of being swept off her feet, into uncharted seas. 'N-not now,' she said.

'What are you afraid of? It's not like you.'

Capri tried to smile, but her lips trembled. 'Isn't it? I wouldn't know.'

He regarded her with grave curiosity. 'You don't remember ever making love?'

'No,' she admitted. 'I suppose that seems silly, when you...'

Her voice trailed off. He knew her intimately, had done for more than two years.

'No...it's not silly,' Rolfe said. 'Kind of bizarre, but I find it rather intriguing. Piquant.' His thumb moved on her skin, finding the groove behind her ear, caressing down to the junction of neck and shoulder. Then his hand fell away, picked up one of hers and held it. It was her left hand, and he ran a thumb over the third finger, his head bent.

She looked down too, and was struck by a sudden thought. 'What happened to my ring?' she asked. 'Didn't I have a wedding ring?'

CHAPTER SIX

ROLFE glanced up, his eyes seeming strangely blank, almost opaque, and then returned his attention to her bare fingers. He said flatly, 'You must have lost it in the crash.'

'Would it have been loose?'

He released her and got up. 'You were unconscious when you were found. There will have been a lot of people about—rescuers, other passengers, and probably sightseers and opportunists. You also had a rather expensive engagement ring that may have taken someone's fancy.'

'You think my rings were *stolen*!' Her skin crawled at the idea of some heartless thief taking them from her finger while she lay injured—for all they knew, dying. 'That's horrible!'

'I'll buy you replacements.'

'That's not the point!'

'No, it isn't,' he agreed. 'But we'll do it all the same.' Changing the subject, he said, 'What have you been doing with yourself?'

'I went into the...my workroom and tried the computer, but I can't even remember how to work the design program.' She made a helpless little gesture.

'Don't force it,' he said. 'Isn't that what they told you?'

'Yes.' She looked about the coolly elegant room. 'I thought being in familiar surroundings would help, but they're not familiar at all. Nothing seems to belong.' She lifted her eyes. 'You're the only thing that's clear in my mind, the only thing I can...cling to.'

Swift compassion entered his eyes. 'Any time.' He went down on his haunches and grasped her hand again. 'I'm here for you, Capri. We'll get you through this.'

'You're being very patient.'

'Maybe I could have been more patient in the past. I'm doing my best.'

'I know.' Her fingers curled about his. She tried to push from her mind a frightening suspicion that he'd come for her and taken her home only because he'd been left little choice. That their marriage had been disintegrating. 'I'm grateful,' she told him.

'You're my wife, Capri. That means a lot to me. More than I ever realised.'

Her head lifted and she searched his face. Surely that comment was right from his heart, not some empty reassurance. She remembered the look on his face when she'd first said she wanted to go home—and her momentary conviction that she had only to give the word and he'd have whisked her away with him there and then. The almost covetous way he sometimes stared at her, and his kisses—tender, possessive, passionate. And his frustration when she'd stopped him making love to her in the kitchen, frustration spilling over briefly into anger. She couldn't doubt that he wanted her.

But then, men sometimes wanted where they didn't love. And love was more important...more lasting and true than desire on its own.

Perhaps Rolfe sensed her doubts. He said slowly, 'After they called for me to come to the hospital I was in some kind of limbo, unable to think, to feel... When I saw you lying there unconscious, looking so frail and still...what I felt was far too complicated to put into words. Waiting for you to wake, I ran through a lifetime of emotions, remembering everything we'd shared since the moment we met.'

'You were angry,' she remembered.

After a tiny pause he admitted, 'I was angry that you'd gone off on your own and got hurt, angry that I'd let you do it—that I'd driven you away, been insensitive to your needs, that I'd never realised how very insecure you were under all your sophistication and apparent self-confidence. Angry at the whole damn world and what had happened to you...to us. And I was scared for you, and saddened, remorseful...you name it. I had plenty of time to think while I watched you and waited and dreaded and hoped. And made silent promises to you—and to myself. When I turned round and you had opened your eyes at last, you looked at me with something like wonder, a sort of innocent recognition and...it was as if we were meeting for the first time all over again.'

'For me too,' she reminded him, smiling to chase away the lump in her throat. 'But I'd like to be able to remember that first time.'

His hand on hers tightened. 'It'll happen. Have you spoken to your mother?'

'I don't know the number.'

'Hell!' Closing his eyes, Rolfe shook his head. 'I should have thought—'

'It's not your fault, Rolfe. I might have remembered, just as I remembered my birth-date and my sister's name—and you. But I don't. I did look—'

'I have it in my electronic organiser,' he said. 'It shouldn't be too late.' He stood up. 'You can use the phone in my office.'

The organiser was in the briefcase that now stood on his desk. He dialled the number for her and said,

'Treena? Rolfe… Yes, she's okay—well, almost. She's right here… Of course you can speak to her.'

He handed Capri the portable receiver and pulled out the chair from behind the desk for her before leaving the room.

'Hello?' she said tentatively. 'Mum?'

'Capri!' a voice screeched into her ear. 'Darling! Are you all *right*?'

Blank surprise held her silent for a moment, until Treena repeated, *'Capri?'*

'Yes, I'm all right,' she said hastily. This was her mother's voice? She'd expected some shock of recognition, perhaps even a miraculous restoration of memory.

'I've been so *worried*!'

Numbly she replied, 'You needn't be, really. Rolfe just told you, I'm fine, except—'

'Except? *Except what?* What have you *done*?'

'Done?' A faint amusement stirred. As if she'd *caused* the train crash? 'I had bruising and a bang on the head—'

'Rolfe told us *that*!'

'And—um—I've lost a large part of my memory.'

As Capri shifted the phone an inch away from her ear the voice lifted higher. 'You've *lost* your *memory*?'

'The doctors say it will almost certainly come back eventually.'

'You don't remember *anything*?'

'Some things,' Capri temporised. 'I knew Rolfe when I saw him, but I don't remember our wedding. And… until Rolfe mentioned it I'd forgotten that you'd moved to America.' And forgotten her mother's name. Treena. 'I remembered Venetia, though. How is she?'

'Excited. She's got a part in a film—a supporting part, but quite a good role.'

'That's wonderful! Tell her congratulations.'

'Well, that's *nice* of you, Capri! Are you *really* going to be all right?'

'I'm sure I will be,' Capri lied valiantly. 'I feel perfectly healthy, only a bit tired. It's just this thing with my memory is...inconvenient.'

'Are you *sure* you shouldn't still be in the hospital? I don't like the sound of this at all!'

'I've been checked and tested over and over. They wouldn't have let me leave if they'd thought there was anything seriously wrong.'

'You look *after* yourself and make sure that husband of yours does too.'

'He's being very considerate,' Capri said quickly.

'Well, good! Make the most of it while you can.'

'While I can?'

'It might not last. Don't count on it.'

At a loss, Capri asked, 'What do you mean?'

'Just that *men*...you know. Once the gloss wears off... You've been married for...what, two years now?'

'Is that what happened to you and...and my father? The gloss wore off?'

'Oh, Capri, you *know* what happened—or maybe you don't any more. Well, if that bastard is wiped out of your memory I can only say good riddance. I'm not going to talk to you about *him*.'

Apparently she'd touched a still-raw nerve. 'I didn't mean to upset you.'

'I'm happy now for the first time in *years*,' Treena said. 'I hoped you'd be happy for me too.'

'I am. I mean, I'm sure I am,' Capri said, feeling that the conversation was taking a surreal turn. 'I'm very glad.'

'You are? Well, just try to *remember* that when you get your memory back.'

'Yes.' Questions whirled in her head, but before she could choose one, discarding those that seemed utterly tactless, Treena said she'd been on her way out and maybe Capri could call back tomorrow.

'Yes,' Capri agreed. 'It's been nice talking to you. Give my regards to...I'm sorry, I don't remember my stepfather's name.'

A peal of laughter came down the line. 'Well, that's the first time you've called Steve *that*!'

'Is it?' Capri enquired blankly.

'Never mind, I'm sure he'll be *tickled* to have your regards,' Treena said kindly.

Capri put down the receiver and sat blankly staring into space, feeling empty and alone.

Several minutes later Rolfe tapped on the door and came in. 'Finished already?' he asked.

'She had to go out. Rolfe—don't I get on with my family?'

'What makes you ask that?'

'She...my mother seemed surprised that I even asked after my...her husband. And Venetia—she's got a part in a film and when I said to pass on my congratulations I had the impression that they'd be...unexpected. Why would that be?'

Rolfe crossed the room and came round to perch against the desk, looking down at her. 'You were seventeen when your mother remarried, and—I gather—not prepared to accept a stepfather.'

'And Venetia?'

'She was younger, and seemed to take the new marriage more easily. You were the one who was...'

'Was what? Jealous? Upset?'

'Insecure, I guess,' Rolfe said slowly. 'That must have been what was at the root of your opposition. I suppose you were afraid of losing your mother's affection.'

'How did they meet—my mother and stepfather?'

'You had entered a Face of the Year contest run by an Australian women's magazine. The winner was offered a contract with an agency in L.A. Another girl won, but the agency was taken with your photo and offered you an audition. The contest organisers made a special payment to help out with the cost and Treena took you and Venetia over there. I believe it was a very exciting time.'

It would have been for any seventeen-year-old, Capri imagined. She wished she could remember it.

'Then your mother met Steve. She says he could have helped your career, but you felt he was trying to organise your life and you resented it. By the time we met, you were sharing a flat with a couple of girlfriends.'

'So what were you doing in Los Angeles?'

'Drumming up business. A contact invited me to a corporate cocktail party and...there you were.'

'How long were you in America?'

'Three weeks. You and I spent every spare moment together, and after I came home I phoned you daily. We arranged to meet in Hawaii and had a week's holiday together—couldn't get enough of each other. Afterwards I persuaded you to come to New Zealand with me, and a couple of months later we were married.'

'What about my career?'

'You seemed to think that being married to me was worth giving it up for.' His mouth curved into a wry smile. 'Incredibly flattering.'

She must have been very much in love. Falling into bed on their very first meeting, flying off to Hawaii for

a snatched idyll. Giving up her career at the drop of a
hat. 'What *was* I doing in Australia?' she asked. 'It
wasn't just a holiday, was it? Why was it so important
that I wouldn't even wait for you to come with me? That
I'd fight over it with you and go off in a huff, even let
you think I might have left for good.'

Rolfe looked past her to the window, taking his time.

'It must have been important to me,' she said, 'whatever it was.'

'You were hoping to look someone up,' he told her
at last.

'A friend? Family?'

He made an odd little grimace. 'Family.'

'I have relatives in Australia? Did they know I was
on that train? Will they be worried?'

'It seems not. No one enquired after the accident, and
the disaster was widely publicised in Australia—even
here. Maybe you never found them after all.'

'In two months? But didn't I have an address?'

'No.' Rolfe straightened away from the desk. 'No, I
don't believe you had a current address.'

'Then I can't have been close to them. Who...?'

The obvious answer came to her. She should have
guessed earlier, of course. 'It was my father, wasn't it?
I was hoping to find him. I went there to look for my
father.'

Rolfe didn't reply immediately, and she remembered,
'My mother says he's a bastard.'

He seemed almost nonplussed. Then a strange, wary
expression entered his eyes. 'You remember her saying
that?'

'She said it just now, on the phone. Is she right?'

'I never met the man,' Rolfe told her, still with that
wary look, his voice very even. 'I expect she's biased,

but I don't have much time myself for men who abandon their families.'

'Is that why you didn't want me to go? You didn't think he was worth the trouble?'

His answer didn't come immediately. 'I never said I didn't want you to, only that perhaps you should have given it some more thought before rushing off to…to hunt for some unknown relative who might not want to be found. Anyway,' he added on a much more brusque note, 'it seems that your quest was unsuccessful. For now, I think you should concentrate on getting over the accident. You still look a bit paler than I think is good for you.'

Capri got up from the chair. 'Did you want to work here?'

'I should.' He looked rueful. 'It wasn't the best time to take off at a moment's notice, workwise.'

'I'm sorry.' She moved around the desk, then paused before going to the door, lifting her face to look at him. 'I found my picture in your drawer, when I was hunting for my mother's phone number. Did you put it away when I left?' Had he really thought she wasn't coming back?

His quick frown made her wonder if he was annoyed at her having rifled through his desk. He forced a smile. 'I've accidentally knocked it off a couple of times, moving things about. Giving it to me was a nice thought, but photos on a business desk are a bit impractical.'

'I gave it to you?'

'A first anniversary present.'

'What did you give me?'

'A silver and sapphire bracelet that you fancied. And flowers—roses. You took your jewellery box with you, by the way. I'm afraid it hasn't turned up.'

Sapphires would have been valuable. And perhaps there had been other items of value as well. And if she had taken jewellery he'd given her, surely she'd had every intention of returning? 'Did you tell the police they were missing?'

'I filled in forms. But it's not important alongside the fact of your survival.'

'Thank you, Rolfe. You are a nice man!'

He looked uncomfortable. 'Not always.'

'Well, I think you are.' She was only a couple of feet away from him. Stepping forward, she leaned up and shyly kissed his cheek. 'What time would you like dinner?'

He grabbed her arms before she could retreat, his clasp hard, then easing as though he realised he was holding her too tightly. His thumbs made tiny caressing movements on her skin, and he gave her a crooked little smile, his eyes softening. 'Are you cooking?' He sounded sceptical, as if the offer was unexpected.

'Why not? There's plenty of food in the kitchen.'

His hands slid down to hers, briefly holding them before he released her. 'Well...' He glanced at his watch. 'About seven, then? Don't tire yourself.'

Rolfe came into the kitchen as she picked up a small bowl of chopped ingredients and dropped them into a pot at the stove before replacing the bowl on the counter. She grasped the handle of the pot, gently shaking the contents.

'Something smells nice.' He leaned over and sniffed, his hand on her waist, barely touching her. So there was no need for the sudden tightening of her skin, the increased flow of blood in her veins.

'I've only just started cooking.'

'I think I meant you.' He snagged her wrist, raising her hand to sniff at her fingers. 'Very savoury.'

'Onions, celery salt and herbs.'

'Delicious.' He dipped his tongue into her palm and she felt the damp rasp of it along her skin to the tips of her fingers.

Capri gasped, and when his hold loosened she reached for a wooden spoon, her fingers shaking as she stirred the onions and herbs.

Rolfe's gaze lifted to her face. 'Did I offend you?'

'No, of course not.' She shook her head.

She hadn't been offended. She'd been aroused. Fiercely and unexpectedly, with a force that had shocked her, sending a jolt of pure sexual sensation through her entire body. Nothing like that had ever happened to her before...

How can you be sure? her mind mocked her. Presumably Rolfe had always woken a similar reaction in her. From the first moment they'd met...

Perhaps subconsciously she recognised his touch, and that was what made her response to him so intense. Yet her instinctive reaction had been to hide from him what he'd done to her with that teasing, sexy caress.

She was married to the man. All she needed to do was follow the dictates of her body, let her feelings have free rein. Why was she afraid to do that?

She pushed back her hair from suddenly hot cheeks. 'I hope you like pasta. I found some in the pantry.' She tipped an already opened can of tomato purée into the pot and stirred it in.

'Yes, I do.' With a small laugh Rolfe added, 'Just as well, as it's about all you ever cook.'

'Really?'

He let his hand slide from her waist and lounged

against the counter near her. 'You look as though you're enjoying yourself. No problems remembering what to do?'

'I just knew without thinking about it.' She peered into the mixture and reached to turn down the heat.

'Want a drink before dinner?' he asked her.

'If you're having one. Thank you. I found the wine rack in the pantry. I've opened a red to let it breathe.'

'You prefer whites.'

'Yes, but the red will go better with this.'

Shortly afterwards he handed her a glass, and she sipped at the cool, refreshing liquid with an underlying bite. 'It's nice. What is it?'

'Your usual. Gin with lemon and bitters.' He picked up the drink he'd poured for himself. 'Shall we have these on the terrace, or do you need to keep an eye on the food?'

'It's ready now, but it can stand for ten minutes.'

They sat at a small table, looking over the water as it flattened and silvered. Capri held her glass in both hands, keeping her gaze on the view. What did one talk about with a husband one knew next to nothing about? But who presumably knew a lot about her.

'What are you thinking?' Rolfe asked softly.

Capri took a quick sip of her drink. 'That you know me much better than I feel I know you.'

'What do you want to know?'

She looked at him then. 'You don't mind?'

'Of course I don't mind.' He raised his glass to his lips, drank, and then put it down.

'You have a family?'

'Yes, I do. My parents live in Tauranga—'

'That's on the coast further south?'

'Right. I have a brother in the States, teaching school

in Pennsylvania. He has an American wife and two children. My sister is in New Zealand, a full-time mother right now, married to a doctor practising in the South Island.'

'Where do you come in the family?'

'I'm the middle one.' He grinned and lifted his drink to his lips again. 'They say it makes you competitive.'

'Are you? Competitive?'

'I suppose. I used to enjoy playing rugby, but I gave it up after university to put all my energies into developing my business.'

'You're single-minded.'

Rolfe shrugged, smiling slightly. 'That, too. I've had to be, to build Massey Laser Systems up from scratch in less than ten years. It's been a hard grind, but worth it in the end.'

'The business is obviously successful.' When his brows lifted enquiringly, she looked about them. 'This house—it must have cost a lot of money.'

'We can afford it. Yes, the business is doing well, but that doesn't mean I can relax. There are always others ready to leap into any gap in the market.'

'Atianui looks...affluent.'

'Most people here are in business or the professions, leavened by the folk who've retired here, some of them ex-farmers. There's a fairly lively social life. Plenty of parties.'

'I don't think I want to go to any parties just now.'

'No reason why you should.' Rolfe drained his glass and put it down. 'You needn't be afraid that I'll force you into anything, Capri. You do understand that?'

She looked at him, flushing under his steady gaze. 'Thank you.'

He moved abruptly, pushing back his chair. 'Have you finished? I'm hungry.'

Over dinner they talked about the news in the paper he'd left on the table that morning and that she'd perused in the afternoon, and Rolfe told her about the community they lived in, and people he worked with. She listened carefully, but was unable to conjure up faces to fit the names he mentioned.

As he helped her clear away the dishes he said he'd brought some work home so he didn't need to go to the factory the next day. She knew that was because he didn't want to leave her alone. The thought warmed her.

They watched television for a while, and then Capri murmured that she'd like to go to bed.

Rolfe stood up, caught her hand in his and drew her to him. Lifting his other hand, he touched her hair, tucking a strand back from her cheek. He bent and kissed her, slow and sweet and restrained, sending delicious thrills coursing through her limbs.

It was over too quickly. He released her and said, 'Have a good night's rest.'

'Goodnight, Rolfe.' Maybe in the morning she'd wake up and find everything back in place, making sense. Maybe.

It didn't happen. Her mind was as blank as before, except for events that had taken place after she woke up in the hospital.

Over breakfast with Rolfe she tried to be cheerful and natural. Afterwards he went to his office down the passageway, telling her to call if she wanted him. 'Can you find things to do?' he enquired.

'I'd like to explore the beach this morning.'

For a moment she thought he was going to object.

Then he said, 'Sure. Better not leave it too late. The sun might seem deceptively mild at this time of year but it could get hot later on, and you don't want to be burnt.'

Except for a lone fisherman in the distance to the right, the smooth pale sand was deserted despite the houses all along the uneven bank above it. Capri turned to the left.

The faint breeze off the sea raised gooseflesh on her arms below the short-sleeved shirt she wore with her jeans, but the sun soon warmed her.

The beach was a broad curve of sand and the water rippled in discreetly, well-behaved waves that left foamy bubbles behind.

She walked at a leisurely pace, stopping now and then to pick up an interesting shell or admire a graceful, hardy plant rooted in the sand, or watch a sea-bird swoop to the water.

The beach ended at a grey rocky outcrop. Finding a handy flat place, she sat for a while, hoping the water and the silence would lull her into a state of calm reverie, but her mind seemed filled with images of Rolfe. None of them was from the time before she woke up in the hospital. After a while she got up and slowly retraced her steps.

Along the foreshore a few old, modest houses recalled the sleepy hollow that Atianui must have been before it became the retreat for the well-heeled that it was now. The newer buildings showed all the signs of architect design and plenty of money.

She was admiring one with a curving front wall of corrugated iron painted aqua-green and echoing the colours and fluidity of the sea, when a man came hurrying down the sandy bank from the two-storeyed ochre cement mansion next door.

He was tall and fair and good-looking. Tight jeans
sheathed his lean hips and a white T-shirt hugged his
well-developed chest.

'Capri!' He waved, and ran lightly across the sand,
blue eyes devouring her all the while. 'Capri, you're
back! I heard you'd been in that train crash in Australia.'

He reached her and grasped her shoulders, apparently
not noticing her instinctive recoil. 'Why didn't you call
me? Are you okay?' he asked her, the vivid eyes searching her face. 'I've been so worried.'

'I'm okay,' she said automatically, detaching herself
with a little difficulty from his hold. 'I was lucky. I'm
sorry…I…do I know you?' she blurted out.

'Know me?' The man blinked, then laughed uncertainly.

'I'm sorry,' she repeated. 'I was injured in the crash
and it's affected my memory. Forgive me, but I don't
remember you at all.'

'You don't *remember* me?' He stared at her. 'Darling,
I'm Gabriel! Gabriel Blake?'

He waited for her to make the connection. Absurdly,
she had an impulse to say, How do you do? Instead she
shook her head in polite regret.

'I don't believe this,' the man said. 'Are you playing
one of your games with me?'

'I'm not playing,' she said thinly. 'I have amnesia.'

'*Amnesia!*'

'I'm afraid so. I really don't have any idea who you
are. Obviously we knew each other—'

His eyes glittered. 'Knew each other? God, yes! We
knew each other very well, darling—biblically.'

The world seemed to rock. She felt her temples grow
cold. Biblically?

Sexually.

CHAPTER SEVEN

IT COULDN'T be true.

'No!' Instinctively she denied the implication.

Gabriel Blake stared at her. 'You're serious, aren't you?' he said at last. 'You really don't remember me?'

Capri moistened her lips. 'I remember very little of my life before the accident. We're hoping it will… improve.'

'We? That husband of yours—did you remember him?'

'Yes.' It was a relief to be able to say so.

His face darkened stormily. 'But not me.'

'I'm sorry,' she heard herself say again.

'Nothing?' He frowned, glanced over his shoulder, and lifted his hands to take her face between them, then brought his mouth down to hers.

She pulled violently away. 'Please don't touch me!'

His face flushed and his lips took on a stubborn pout. 'That's not what you used to say! What the hell's got into you?'

'I told you! I…I don't remember you.' Distractedly she pushed back her hair. 'Look, if you'll excuse me, I really want to go home.'

'Well, don't let me stop you.' He stepped aside, his face the picture of chagrin.

But she had hardly passed him when he said, 'Capri!'

Reluctantly she turned, and he came close to her again. The anger had left his face. 'If this is true, just remember I'm here if you need me.' He touched her arm, then let his hand drop to his side. 'I love you. More than Rolfe ever did.'

'He's being very good to me.'

Gabriel's lips curled disdainfully. His gaze suddenly sharpened. 'You're not sleeping with him, are you? That bastard hasn't wormed his way back into your bed?'

'He's my husband.' She was trembling again.

'Does that mean you *are* sleeping with him?' His voice had risen.

Blood thrummed at her temples. 'It's none of your business!'

She backed from him, but he came after her, seizing her arms again. 'How much do you remember of your relationship with *him*?' he asked fiercely. 'Did he tell you the two of you haven't shared a bed in *months*?'

'Let me go!' She struggled out of his grasp and ran. The soft sand impeded her, and gradually she slowed to a walk, glancing behind her to see Gabriel Blake standing where she had left him, frustration in every line of his body. At the far end of the beach the hopeful fisherman still stood with his rod and line.

Her heart beat uncomfortably fast, and there was a suffocating feeling in her throat.

Had she been having an affair behind Rolfe's back?

Every instinct rejected against the idea. But she had no idea what kind of relationship her marriage had been. Or what other relationships she might have had.

Even adulterous ones?

What would have led her to that?

Rolfe had been kind, patient—loving—since she'd left the hospital. Yet she sensed that something had been amiss in their marriage, and Rolfe admitted he'd been blind to her needs. More than once she'd seen glimpses of some latent anger in him. What might he do if that anger was unleashed, no longer hidden behind a façade of concern and consideration?

Had he driven her into another man's arms?

Unfair, she acknowledged immediately, ploughing her way up the sandy bank before the house. If she was an unfaithful wife, the guilt was hers. But she found it impossible to believe she'd ever cheated on him.

Why should Gabriel Blake lie? That made no sense. He'd been genuinely shocked, she was sure, at her blank non-recognition, and he'd hardly had time to think up a story like that. Besides, what possible reason would he have to do so?

At the door she took off her sand-covered canvas pumps and shook them out before entering the house. Everything was quiet. If she hadn't left Rolfe in his office she'd have thought she was alone.

Should she confront him with her disturbing new… knowledge?

It wasn't knowledge, it was hearsay.

Everything in her rejected the possibility that it might be true, and yet she had no defence, no way to prove her innocence.

Hesitantly, she walked along the passageway and paused at the office door before tapping on the panel.

It was a moment before Rolfe called, 'Come in.'

His gaze was fixed on the screen of the computer on his desk, but he looked up at her and smiled. 'How was your walk?'

'All right. It's a long beach.'

The smile fading, Rolfe said, 'You look a bit whacked. You walked too far.' He got up to come round the desk.

Capri advanced into the room and stood with her

hands gripping the back of an upholstered visitor's chair that stood between them. 'I…met someone.'

'One of the neighbours?'

'I suppose so. Gabriel Blake.'

'Oh, Gabriel.' A faintly contemptuous note entered his voice. Was it her imagination, or had his eyes sharpened under the watchful lids? He stepped closer and rested his own hand on the chair-back. Capri removed hers.

Rolfe frowned. 'Has meeting him upset you?'

'Why should it upset me?' She was hedging, feeling her way.

His eyes searched hers, and she looked away. 'Did you know him?'

Capri shook her head.

'Then at a guess,' he said grimly, 'I'd say you felt somewhat…awkward.'

He told me we'd been having an affair. She looked at her husband's face and swallowed the words. Even if it was true, the last person to ask must surely be Rolfe. If he didn't know, it would be a cruel blow to a man who had shown her nothing but tenderness and understanding since… Well, she thought wryly, ever since she could remember. Stalling again, she asked, 'What do you know about him?'

Rolfe retreated to lean on the desk, folding his arms. 'He's an artist, of sorts.'

'Of sorts?'

'He has family money—at least so I've been told— and he's able to please himself about how often and how hard he works. I believe he's talented, but I have the feeling he might do better if he didn't have the cushion of wealth to fall back on.'

'You think all artists should be starving in garrets?'

Rolfe gave a short laugh. 'I guess I may have a slight bias.'

'Oh...? Why?' She watched him cautiously.

'Maybe because I'm jealous.'

Capri's heart gave one hard thud. 'Jealous?' she repeated uncertainly.

Shrugging, Rolfe straightened, picked up a hexagonal glass paperweight from the desk, inspected it as if he'd never seen it before, and put it down again. 'I've worked like a dog for what I've got and he doesn't need to. Mean-spirited of me, isn't it?'

Watching the self-deprecating smile in his eyes, she said, 'I don't think you're a mean-spirited man, Rolfe.'

'Thank you.' He came closer to her, and touched her cheek. 'You're being very sweet these days, Capri.'

His hand lingered, and she suppressed an urge to turn her head and nestle her cheek into his palm. 'Wasn't I, before?'

The smile deepened, and he slipped his hand under her hair, his fingers gently massaging her skin. 'I certainly thought so when we met.'

'And...later?'

He looked rueful. 'We had our ups and downs, like every married couple. It takes time to adjust to each other. But I'm sure your essential nature hasn't changed.'

She was sure of it too. Which made it all the more puzzling that she felt such revulsion at the idea that she might have deceived him with Gabriel Blake. If she felt this way now, what could have led her to enter into an adulterous affair?

Consumed by a wave of guilt, and afraid of what Rolfe might read in her eyes, she lowered her lashes and stirred under his hand.

He dropped it and stood back. 'What are you planning to do now?'

'I don't know. Would you like me to make you a coffee? It must be morning tea time.'

'I don't often bother with it. But thanks all the same.'

'What about lunch?'

He hesitated. 'I'll join you. About twelve-thirty, all right?'

'I'll make something.'

'Thank you.'

He seemed surprised, and she asked, 'Don't I usually?'

Rolfe smiled. 'Not usually, no.'

'What do we do, then?'

'You generally have fruit and yoghurt, or go out to lunch with a woman friend. And I make myself a cheese or ham sandwich. Sometimes we used to go down the road and have lunch together at the garden centre café when I was home, but I don't suppose—'

'That sounds nice.' She vaguely recalled seeing a garden centre as they drove into town, with a display of pink and red impatiens along the road frontage shaded by silver birches. 'Did we do that often—have lunch there?'

'Not so much lately.'

'There'll be people I know—used to know—there?'

He hesitated. 'Very possibly.'

The thought was a little nerve-racking, but if she didn't try to stimulate her wayward memory what hope did she have of it ever functioning normally again? 'There's no point in skulking about the house, avoiding contact with other people.'

And right now, with the disturbing disclosure that she was possibly an unfaithful wife lodged like a thorn in her mind, the prospect of lunching with Rolfe alone was almost alarming. She had a quite irrational fear of blurting out something she might regret. 'But perhaps you don't have the time?' she suggested.

'That's okay,' he said at last. 'We'll go to the café if it's what you'd like.'

She made herself a coffee while she went uneasily over and over the morning's brief conversation with Gabriel Blake.

He'd been her lover, he said.

He was a handsome man, and obviously capable of passion. And of gentleness. He'd been angry and incredulous that she didn't remember him, but later had offered help, reminded her he'd be there for her if she needed him. Said he loved her.

A volatile person, she guessed, one who might be wildly attractive to certain types of women.

Her type of woman?

Again she slammed up against that wall. What sort of woman *was* she?

Could she be deceitful, disloyal, capable of lying to her husband, of secretly sleeping with another man?

Somewhere in the distance a bell burred. Uncertainly, Capri left the kitchen to make her way to the main door.

Rolfe came out of his office, a slightly harassed look on his face.

'I'll get it,' she told him.

She opened the door to an elderly couple, the woman small and white-haired, the man taller but stooped, both regarding her through identical gold-rimmed spectacles.

The woman held a bouquet of mixed garden flowers, the man a basket full of fruit.

'There you are, dear!' the woman said, beaming. 'You're up and about, then.'

'Yes,' Capri agreed.

'We heard you'd been in that dreadful train crash. We thought you might like some flowers and fruit from our garden.' She held out the flowers.

Capri accepted them, sniffing the mixed perfumes. 'That's very kind.'

'Not at all,' the elderly man said. 'What are neighbours for?'

'Oh, you're neighbours?'

The two exchanged a glance. 'Fred and Myra Venables, dear,' the woman said. 'From across the way.'

'Please, do come in.' Capri stepped back invitingly, clutching the flowers. 'I've just made coffee—perhaps you'd like some.'

After she'd seen the couple off almost an hour later, she found a vase for the flowers and placed them on one of the tables in the lounge. She stood for a while before the big window, contemplating the hypnotic beauty of the sea, then went along to her bedroom to freshen up and change from jeans into a dress.

She was emerging when Rolfe came out of his office again, his eyes taking in the figure-skimming green cotton dress that he'd bought for her. 'I'll just be a few minutes.'

When he rejoined her, smelling of a fresh, woody soap or aftershave, he put a light hand on her back and guided her to the door. 'I suppose you wouldn't like to walk?' He glanced down at her high-heeled cream leather sandals.

'I could change my shoes. How far is it?'

'About ten minutes away on foot.'

'I'll change.'

'Are you sure?'

'I'll only take a minute,' she promised.

She came back in thirty seconds, with the bronze low-heeled pumps on her feet.

'You had visitors,' he said as he closed the door behind them.

'Mr and Mrs Venables.'

'You coped all right? They're a nice old couple, although I know you think they're a nosy pair.'

'They take an interest in what's going on, but I don't think they'd indulge in vicious gossip. They brought me flowers and fruit. Have you got a lot of work done this morning?'

'A fair amount. You haven't had another go at your design program?'

'No.' She'd had no desire to try.

'You always did work in fits and starts,' he assured her. 'When you have a new idea maybe you'll pick it up again quite easily.'

'Maybe,' she echoed.

They reached the bower-like café set among flowers and trees, an obviously popular venue for lunches.

'I'll have a wedge of pineapple and sweet potato pie, with a salad,' Rolfe announced after cursorily studying the menu. 'What about you?' he queried across the table. 'The smoked salmon and asparagus roll?'

'How did you know?' Capri asked, having just made up her mind.

'It's what you nearly always order here.'

'Am I that predictable?'

'Sometimes you surprise me.' He paused. 'A lot, these last few days.'

The waitress took the order and bustled away. Capri

looked about, studying the faces of the other patrons intently.

'Anyone you know?' Rolfe was watching her with almost equal intentness.

She shook her head.

'Don't sweat it,' he said easily. 'There's no rush.'

'Capri!' A feminine voice intruded. 'Capri—I didn't know you were home! How are you?'

A tall, very pretty brunette accompanied by a stocky, balding man stopped beside them.

As Capri looked up Rolfe reached over the table and grasped one of her hands in his. 'Hello, Thea. Capri is still recovering from the accident, but—'

The woman glanced at him and turned again to Capri. 'It must have been awful, you poor thing! But you're looking good.'

'It's affected her memory,' Rolfe explained. 'Capri, Thea and Ted are good friends of ours.'

'Oh, she can't have forgotten us!' The woman peered at Capri.

'I'm afraid so,' Capri confessed. 'It's supposed to be a short-term thing.'

'Good heavens! That's *awful*!' Thea was obviously shocked, and stood awkwardly, at a loss for what to say next.

The waitress arrived with the meals, and Ted drew Thea away, promising to 'Catch up with you later'.

'You all right?' Rolfe asked.

Her smile was lifeless. 'Yes. It's going to happen fairly often, isn't it?'

'Shall I spread the word so we don't need to explain all the time?'

'I think Mr and Mrs Venables might do that for us. In the nicest possible way.' They'd been all clucking sympathy this morning, without disguising their natural curiosity.

'You could be right.' Laughter wiped the habitually vigilant look from his face. She smiled at him, her spirits lifting.

A flare of awareness lit his eyes, and a tautness settled about his cheekbones.

Catching her breath, she dragged her gaze away, pretending to be absorbed in the food on her plate.

They ate without talking much, and when she'd declined a sweet and they'd had coffee, Rolfe pushed back his chair. 'Shall we go?'

'All right.' She cast a wistful look at the inviting gravel paths dividing neatly sorted rows of plants outside.

'You want to look around?' Rolfe asked.

'Do you have time?'

'I'm my own boss. Not too long, though.'

They strolled along the paths, pausing often to admire a flowering shrub or one with particularly pretty foliage. She knew the names of some, but a couple of times she had to inspect the labels.

'You're having quite a good time, aren't you?' Rolfe commented as she turned the label on a six-foot prunus smothered in pink blossom.

'Are you bored?' she asked him anxiously. 'I'm sorry—do you want to go?'

'No.' He shook his head and gave her a rather quizzical look. 'No, I'm enjoying watching you. It's as if it's all new to you. Or you're seeing it through different eyes.'

'It is new. I mean, it seems new. So I suppose I am. Isn't this beautiful?' She looked up at him, her hand still on the label as she stood against the branches with their fragile blooms.

His eyes seemed to glaze as he looked at her, and an almost wistful expression crossed his face. Without moving his gaze from her he said quietly, 'Yes, very beautiful.'

The moment seemed to stretch, the chatter and clattering crockery from the café, the crunch of feet on the gravel paths receding, so she heard only the sound of a bird's trill somewhere nearby, and her own quickened breath.

Rolfe reached up a hand and she felt his fingers in her hair, then he took it away as another couple came down the path towards them, and she saw that he held one of the blossoms from the tree on his palm. It must have fallen on her hair. The other couple reached them, Rolfe moved aside to let them pass, and the moment shattered as he shoved his hands into his pockets.

When they finally left Capri was carrying a terracotta pot holding a miniature rosebush with dusky dark-pink blooms.

'I'll take it,' he offered.

'No, it's not heavy. Thank you, Rolfe.' She bent to sniff at the spicy-sweet perfume. 'It's lovely.'

'I could see you were taken with it.' She had been admiring it when he picked it up and took it to the counter.

'Have you always spoiled me like this?' She smiled up at him.

He looked almost bemused, staring back at her. 'I don't think you thought I was spoiling you. You weren't always so…'

'So—what?' she asked when he paused there.

'So…easily pleased,' he said slowly.

Had she been very demanding before? 'I might have died in that crash,' she said soberly. 'I suppose it's given me a different outlook on life.'

'I suppose it would,' he agreed, his glance speculative. 'They say near-death experiences alter people profoundly.'

Rolfe returned to his study, and Capri tried the potted rose in different spots on the patio, finally settling it against one side of the archway outside the main room. Perhaps she'd buy another to match.

At a loose end after that, she wandered into what she couldn't help thinking of as the sewing room. Poking about rather aimlessly, she found a sketchpad and pencils, and a box full of pastels. The pad was hardly used, only the first two pages carrying some unfinished fashion sketches.

Ripping out the pages, she left them, taking the pad with her to the patio. Picking up the rose in its pot, she placed it on the table, studying it. Then she settled into a chair, her feet propped on the edge of the table, and began drawing.

'Flower pictures?' Rolfe's voice made her jump.

She looked up at him, a pink pastel in her hand. 'Do you like it?'

She'd drawn the rosebush on the table top against the background of blue sky and sea, framed in the white archway. Now she was carefully shading in the petals.

'I like it a lot,' he said. His hands descended lightly on her shoulders. 'Why flowers?'

'I just felt like drawing them.' She put down the pad and replaced the pastel in its box, rubbing at the soft powdery colour on her fingers. 'Did you want me?'

'Yes.'

She swung her feet to the ground and tipped back her head to look at him properly.

When she saw what was in his face she flushed, her eyes widening and lips parting in surprise.

Rolfe removed his hands. 'Don't look so startled. I'm not going to drag you off to bed against your will, but I can't pretend I wouldn't like to.'

'Well, you did startle me,' she returned. She'd seen the naked desire in his eyes before he masked it, reminding her forcefully that her first impression of him had been of a man who was aware of and enjoyed his own sexuality. 'You know that wasn't what I meant!'

He gave her a crooked grin of acknowledgement and came round the table to drop into the chair opposite hers. 'Point taken.' He reached out to touch the rose, and grimaced in pain. 'Damn.'

As he pulled back his hand, ruefully inspecting his thumb, she got up. 'Let me see.'

She held his wrist and peered at the tiny droplet of blood that broke through the skin. 'Do you have a thorn in there?'

'Feels like it.' He took back his hand and sucked at the blood, then looked again. 'Mm, I can see it, I think.'

Capri reclaimed his hand. 'Keep still.' Carefully she pinched the barely visible black end between her fingernails and pulled it out. 'There.'

'Thank you.' He slid his other arm about her waist and drew her down onto his knee. 'You could kiss me better.'

'Could I?' She peeked at him, stupidly shy but intrigued at the idea of taking the initiative.

One large hand ruffled her hair. 'If you like,' he invited.

He was leaving it up to her. She would like it, she thought. The warmth of his lap, the faint rise and fall of his chest, the light hold of his arms were seductive, as was the masculine scent of him and the stubble-darkened texture of his cheek, tantalisingly close to hers. Her breathing quickened, a faint, not unpleasant prickling sensation running over her skin.

Temptation mingled with a sense of unease that had lingered ever since that morning's encounter with Gabriel Blake.

'Capri?' Rolfe's voice was a low, enquiring murmur, and his cheek nudged her temple.

She had only to turn her head slightly. A moment longer she hesitated, then did so, tentatively finding his mouth, surprised by its softness. She felt he was holding his breath, and for seconds he didn't respond to her cautious exploration, letting her discover in her own way the feel of his lips, the shape and texture of them against hers.

Then he groaned deep in his throat and his arms tightened, her head was tipped back into the possessive curve of his shoulder and his mouth parted hers in sweet demand.

Even as her heart thudded against her ribs, she knew he was tempering his passion, pacing it to her response. Which she gave with increasing abandon, her body shivering with delicious little hot darts of pleasure as her lips moved under his, following his every lead.

When he finally tore his mouth away one of his hands had found its way inside the bodice of her dress, the buttons undone and her lacy bra exposed, except that his hand covered it, the thumb insistently stroking the warm swell of flesh above the lace. His voice when he spoke was low and rasping. 'If this is going any further we should move inside.'

It was a question, and one that she had to answer. She fleetingly met his blazing eyes, and touched her tongue to lips already moist and throbbing from his kisses.

She wanted to do as he suggested, go inside with him and lose herself in lovemaking, bury her doubts in passion. But the bothersome thought that Gabriel Blake had planted in her mind that morning wouldn't quite go away. *You haven't shared a bed with him in months.*

'Which room?' she heard herself say in guarded tones.

'Which room?' He sounded hazy, as if she'd thrown him off balance.

She pursued the question that now was at the forefront of her mind. 'Yours or mine?'

Rolfe frowned. 'Does it matter?' he enquired curtly.

'I don't know.' Capri swallowed. 'I just wondered...why we have separate rooms at all. Why we haven't been sleeping together.'

She could feel the instant stillness of his body. 'If you remember, you said I was a stranger to you since the accident. I thought you'd prefer a bit of time to adjust.'

He was avoiding the real question. She stirred in his arms, sitting up straighter. 'But there's nothing of yours in that room,' she said. 'We weren't sharing it before.'

His body tensed even further. There was a slight pause before he told her, almost too easily, 'It's no big deal, Capri. We have a large house, and there isn't any law that says we have to share a room.'

'You mean we've always had separate rooms?'

Again he paused. 'When we first moved in we shared. But after a time you preferred to have your own private space. Plenty of married people have separate rooms, for all kinds of reasons. When a husband snores—'

'Do you?'

'Yes.' The reply was too prompt, too pat. 'Yes, that's it.' He met her suspicious gaze with a bland one of his own. 'And you need your sleep, so—'

'I don't believe you.' Abruptly she struggled off his knee and took two steps before turning to face him.

His eyes went to the gaping front of her dress and she hastily drew the edges together, fumbling with the buttons.

He watched as though he couldn't tear his attention away, and not until she'd finished did he look up at her face.

'Don't lie to me, Rolfe.' Her voice shook. 'I'm confused enough as it is, everything's so...'

He got up too, looking both aloof and tense. 'I'm trying to protect you, Capri. Can't you just trust me?'

She wanted to, her instinct said to do so. But she knew he was keeping something from her. She cried in frustration, 'How can I trust you when I hardly know you?'

All expression disappeared from his face as if it had been wiped off.

'I'm sorry,' she said miserably. 'I don't mean to be hurtful, only...'

'You needn't apologise,' he said austerely. 'You're not to blame.'

Tears stung her eyes, and she turned away to hide them from him. The afternoon was waning, the waves already growing lazy and hushed. 'You have to tell me,' she said stubbornly.

'Tell you what?'

'What happened—I need to know the truth about how long we've been sleeping apart from each other. And why.'

Seconds ticked by, and she thought he wasn't going to answer. 'Before you went away?' he said finally, his voice grown hard. 'About four months,' he told her. 'Since shortly after you lost the baby.'

CHAPTER EIGHT

NUMBLY Capri turned to face him.

There was a rushing sound in her ears. Her voice was hushed. 'We had a baby?'

Rolfe's eyes were bleak, and she wondered if he regretted having mentioned it. 'You lost it early in the pregnancy.' He stood unmoving, his face blanked of all expression.

Mentally groping for something to hold on to, Capri asked, 'Were we...had we wanted it?'

'It wasn't exactly planned. You may have forgotten a couple of times to take your pill.'

'How did I lose it?'

'The pregnancy spontaneously aborted when you were scarcely more than two months on.'

'A miscarriage.'

'The doctor said it's not uncommon for a first pregnancy. There's no reason why we shouldn't have perfectly healthy babies in the future, Capri. None.'

'But we were sleeping apart.'

'Having separate bedrooms doesn't necessarily preclude lovemaking,' he said carefully. After a short pause he added, 'I recall several torrid interludes on a blanket on the beach at night. And you've been known to seduce me in my office on more than one occasion...'

Heat throbbed at her cheekbones. There was no reason to be embarrassed, but she was. 'You're right,' she said, cutting off any more revelations, 'I don't remember, and

I don't remember why we decided on separate bedrooms, or what it had to do with the miscarriage.'

His voice was smooth as cream. 'You had trouble sleeping afterwards. I often work late and didn't want to disturb you.'

It was plausible. Yet a nagging unease persisted. Had their marriage been in trouble before the miscarriage—or had the loss itself caused problems?

Rolfe said, 'We can alter the arrangement any time it suits you.' His eyes went again to the front of her dress, now neatly buttoned, and his tone turned sardonic. 'Am I wrong in thinking you've lost the mood for now?'

Briefly she sucked her lower lip. 'No, you're not wrong. I'm sorry.' She felt mixed up and on edge, desperately wanting to accept his explanation. It did, after all, make perfect sense. Except that Gabriel Blake had told her she'd been sleeping with *him*.

If she told Rolfe that, it could widen whatever rift had already existed between them, wreck any chance of saving their relationship. In the hospital she'd glanced at the Agony Aunt column in one of the magazines she'd been given. The advice to a repentant wife had been to keep her infidelity secret, because confessing to her husband might relieve her conscience but would hurt him badly.

Maybe the magazine had contained a hidden message for her.

Rolfe shrugged. 'There'll be other times.'

Other times when he'd want to make love to her, and when she might reciprocate fully. Part of her wanted that very much, yet doubt and a festering sense of guilt held her back.

The telephone rang, and Rolfe went inside to answer it.

Seconds later he called, 'Capri? Your mother.'

She'd forgotten to call. She hurried down the passage-way to the hall phone, and Rolfe passed her the portable receiver and went into his study.

She let Treena do most of the talking. Her mother had an active social life, and was very proud of her younger daughter whose acting career seemed to be taking off. But finally she switched to asking, 'And how are *you*? Is your *memory* improving?'

'Not yet.' Capri suppressed the insidious thought that it might never happen.

'Hasn't *anything* come back to you?'

Capri hesitated. Would she have confided in her mother if she'd been having an extra-marital affair? 'Do you...did I ever mention a Gabriel Blake to you?'

'Who's he?'

'Oh, just a neighbour,' Capri said hastily. 'I met him this morning. And some other neighbours came over,' she tacked on, to lead Treena off the subject. 'Mr and Mrs Venables.'

Treena laughed. 'Oh, you've mentioned *them*. A couple of old stickybeaks, you said.'

Her conscience twinged. 'They're really very nice. Very concerned about me.'

'Most people are nice,' Treena told her, 'if you just give them the *chance*, Capri.'

'I'm sure you're right.'

'I've *always* been right, dear, if only you'd *listen* to me. Now I have to go, but you take care of yourself, you hear?'

Smiling a little, Capri promised she would.

Over dinner with Rolfe she said, 'I must have been a difficult daughter?'

'I don't know if you were any more difficult than

average. Most parents find the teenage years rather trying.'

'Did yours?'

'Probably. My brother worried them by hitchhiking his way around Asia and Europe, before ending up in America with a good steady job and a family.'

'What about you?'

'They thought I was taking a risk going into business on my own when I'd only just left university, but they've always been supportive.'

'Did they lend you money?' He'd been scathing of Gabriel Blake's reliance on family money, but surely his own family must have been comfortably off?

'No,' Rolfe said, dispelling that idea. 'My father worked for wages all his life, and my mother had a part-time job in a supermarket after we kids left primary school. They did without a lot to see the three of us through university so that we'd have a better education than either of them. In the early days of my business they let me fit out their garage as a small laboratory, and even offered to remortgage their house when I was having trouble getting a loan, but I talked a bank into backing me.'

She recalled his confessed envy of Gabriel Blake's reliance on inherited wealth. 'They sound like good people.'

He cast her a quizzical look. 'I think a lot of them.'

'I'd like to—oh. I suppose I have met them. Did you tell them…what's happened?'

'I phoned before we left Australia and again when I brought you home. They'd like to help but I don't imagine there's much they can do.'

'Still, it was nice of them to offer.'

After dinner Rolfe suggested a stroll on the beach before it got dark. He took her hand and she let her fingers lie in his, enjoying the warm, strong clasp.

They met a couple walking a dog and exchanged brief greetings.

'Do we know them?' Capri asked.

'Only by sight. They have a rather striking house with curving walls, coloured in sea-greens and blues.'

'Next door to Gabriel Blake's.'

Rolfe looked at her sharply. 'You remember it?'

'No.' Hastily, she shook her head. 'I told you I met him on the beach. I was looking at that house you just described when he saw me and came...to say hello.' Again she felt guilt tugging at her. 'He'd heard about the accident,' she said.

'It was in the newspapers and on television, and word got around that you'd been in it. A number of our clients have asked how you are, and the workers at the factory enquire after you.'

'That's nice. Do you tell them about the amnesia?'

'No. But it's nothing to be embarrassed about, Capri.'

'I'm not embarrassed. Just frustrated. And sometimes...'

'What?' Rolfe stopped walking and gathered her other hand in his, looking down at her. His face looked shadowed in the gathering dusk.

'Sometimes I feel this awful emptiness, as if my brain is hollowed out, nothing there. What if it never changes, Rolfe? What if my memory never comes right?'

His hands slid up her arms, warming them. 'They said give it time.' He paused. 'But I promised I'd take you to see someone, if it's what you want.'

She sensed reserve in his voice. Maybe he thought she was too impatient. 'Perhaps in a week or two,' she decided, 'if nothing happens.'

'Fine. It's up to you.' Was that relief she heard in his voice? He kissed her forehead, then moved his hands to her waist and pulled her closer, his eyes dark and questioning.

Her heart pounding erratically, she lifted her face, gazing gravely back at him, and waited.

The kiss was warm and exciting, though restrained. She returned it shyly, following his lead. Then a dog barked and Rolfe lifted his head, looking over hers at the people they'd met earlier returning along the beach. Rolfe's arms loosened their hold, but he kept one about her waist as he turned her to keep on walking.

The other couple's pace was much brisker, and they soon passed with a cheerful wave, the dog trotting ahead.

'Goodnight,' the man said, and Rolfe responded.

'They must have seen us,' Capri murmured.

'It isn't illegal to kiss on the beach.' He sounded amused. 'And we are married.'

She thought about the other things he said they'd done on the beach sometimes, after dark, and a hot, delicious shiver coursed through her.

They strolled on, and she saw the couple with the dog leave the sand and climb to their house—the one next door to Gabriel Blake's.

By the time Capri and Rolfe reached the spot there was no sign of anyone about. Rolfe halted, looking up at the house. 'It's quite something, isn't it?'

'Yes,' she agreed. 'Do you know who designed it?'

'I believe their son is an architect.' His arm moved to her shoulders. 'Ready to go back?'

It was rapidly darkening now. 'Mm, maybe we should.' Starting to turn, Capri felt Rolfe's arm tighten as he pulled her into his embrace. His free hand cupped her chin, tipping her head, and his mouth closed over hers in a kiss that was intimate and frankly sensual.

She returned it, more confidently than before, giving him back what he gave her, recognising his arousal with a sense of primitive female triumph that was new to her. His hand slid down, and he hauled her closer to him as his legs parted, trapping her between his thighs, and his blatant arousal sent a bolt of excitement through her body.

Light suddenly beat against her closed lids, making them flutter, her body stiffen, and after a few seconds Rolfe released her mouth, his arms easing about her.

The window of the house to the right of the one they'd been admiring blazed with yellow light. Gabriel Blake's house.

Dizzy and breathless, her skin burning, the adrenalin pumping through her veins, Capri clung to Rolfe, her fingers clutching his shirt as he laid his forehead against hers and said in a low, harsh voice, 'Maybe you weren't ready for that. I'm having difficulty keeping my hands off you, I want you so much. You'll have to tell me if I go too fast.'

I want you too. She almost said the words, but as she moved, trying to look up at him, the lighted window caught her eye again, a shadow moving behind the glass.

Instinctively she pulled away from Rolfe.

He was watching her, but it was almost dark and she could no longer see his expression clearly. Then he turned his head, stared at the lit window and slowly looked back at her.

Capri swung round and began walking back the way they had come, and Rolfe fell into step beside her, possessing her hand again.

She should say something, tell him it was all right, that his kiss had been welcome.

Only she couldn't help wondering if he'd chosen his moment, deliberately pressing that long, very obviously intimate kiss on her in full view of Gabriel Blake.

CHAPTER NINE

WHEN they got back to the house the phone was ringing, and Rolfe hurried to pick it up before the answering machine cut in. Capri could hear him talking as she dusted sand off her shoes and carried them to her room.

She was putting the shoes away when Rolfe tapped on the open bedroom door and walked in. 'That was Thea,' he told her, 'inviting us to a barbecue on Saturday.'

Thea—the dark-haired young woman they'd met at the café. 'There'll be people there that I should know?'

'I said you may not feel up to it but she insists it's just a casual get-together, and I promised to talk to you.'

Turning down the invitation without a real excuse would be rude, and it sounded as though Thea was anxious to have her there. Thea was a friend. Capri probably needed friends to help her piece her life back together. 'I guess we should go. It was good of her to ask.'

'Are you sure? If you don't want to—'

'Hiding in the house won't help bring my memory back.'

After a moment he said, 'Shall I accept, then?'

'I could do it tomorrow if you give me her number.'

'I'll leave it on my desk for you. I have to go to the factory again tomorrow, but Hallie will be here.'

'I really don't need nursemaiding, Rolfe. I'll be fine, with or without Hallie.'

'Still…I prefer knowing you're not alone.'

'It's nice of you to care.'

'I've always cared, Capri. I wish—'

'What?' she asked as he halted.

'I keep forgetting you don't remember things that happened before. I was going to say, I wish I could convince you of how much I care.'

'I know you do.' Whatever problems they might have had, his concern and care had been obvious from the time she woke and saw him in the hospital. He wanted their marriage to work. She had to believe that, *needed* to believe it. Any alternative was too scary to entertain.

She saw his eyes soften, go dark, and he stepped towards her.

'I think I'll have an early night,' she said quickly.

He halted, a few feet away from her. 'Sure,' he said. And then, 'May I kiss you goodnight?'

'You don't need to ask permission, Rolfe.'

He took his time, his hands lightly gripping her shoulders to draw her into his arms. The kiss itself was gentle, his mouth barely brushing hers, leaving her oddly disappointed, yet on another level relieved that he hadn't demanded more.

He eased back and searched her eyes as if something about her both amused and perplexed him. 'Goodnight, my sweet,' he said. Then he released her and turned to walk out of the room.

Hallie was cheerful and brisk, and seemed to find plenty to do even though Capri wondered why they needed her services twice every week. Except for the sand that was no doubt tracked or possibly even blown into the house on occasion, there didn't appear to be much to make it dirty.

Capri telephoned Thea, who was inclined to chat, but they soon ran out of conversation. Capri reflected that it must be difficult trying to talk to someone who didn't remember you or any of the people you mentioned.

Hallie was still busy and, feeling in the way, Capri retreated to the beach with a sketch-book and pencil.

There she sat on the sandbank and drew the marram grass and harestails, stopping now and then to gaze at the ocean and examine the far recesses of her mind for some clue to her former life.

After Hallie had gone Capri made herself a salad sandwich, and was eating it while she read the paper when the telephone rang.

She went down the hall and picked up the receiver, and at her greeting a man's voice said, 'Capri? It's Gabriel. Is Rolfe about?'

'No, but—'

'Can I come and see you?'

Tensely, she answered, 'I don't think that would be a good idea.'

'Capri, you don't understand.'

'I understand that I'm married,' she said firmly, 'and whatever I might have done before—if what you say is true—'

'It's true!' he burst out. 'Look, I know you felt I'd let you down—'

'Why would I feel that?'

'Just let me come round and explain—'

On the point of a firm refusal, she hesitated. What if he held the key to her elusive memories? Supposing he could help her back to normality?

'Are you frightened of your husband?' he demanded.

'Not frightened.' The denial was instinctive, but she certainly didn't fancy Rolfe's possible reaction if he found her enjoying a tête-à-tête with another man. 'I just don't want to…go behind his back.'

'Darling—'

'I don't think you should call me that,' she said sharply.

'All right—*Capri*! If you can't remember what went on between us before, or the state of your marriage, how do you know you didn't have good reason?'

Was there ever a good reason for adultery? Even if Rolfe had beaten her, which she didn't imagine for a minute, she surely should have severed her marriage tie before embarking on a love affair with someone else.

'Look, I'm coming round anyway.' He put down the phone, and Capri replaced the receiver and stood for a while before going outside to the terrace facing the sea. If he was determined, there wasn't much point in barricading herself in the house.

As she'd expected, he came along the beach, bounding up the bank and striding towards her where she stood waiting for him, her hands secretly clenched in the pockets of a bleached linen skirt.

'Capri.' His blue eyes were bright and bold. He seemed about to reach for her but she stepped back quickly, and he made a helpless gesture instead. 'Can't we sit down?'

Stiffly she took one of the chairs flanking the small outdoor table and clasped her hands loosely on the cold surface.

Gabriel sank into the chair opposite, surveying her with those hungry blue eyes, and she stirred uneasily. His shoulders slumped, and he too clasped his hands on the table in front of him, his head bent.

She asked, 'How did you let me down?'

Gabriel looked up. 'I said you *felt* I'd let you down. I had to take a trip to America for an exhibition that had been booked for months—I'm an artist.'

'Yes, Rolfe told me.'

'You've discussed me with him since you came home?'

'We didn't *discuss* you. I mentioned we'd met on the beach.'

'Does he suspect...?'

'I don't think so.' Capri felt acutely uncomfortable. Just sitting here with this man was making her conscience-stricken about something she didn't even remember. 'When...how long were we...did this affair of ours last?'

'We'd been seeing each other for weeks before I flew to New York, and in the last few days...we became lovers. When I came back you'd gone. Rolfe said you were on holiday, but I was sure you'd left him. He'd be too proud to admit it, of course. I waited for you to get in touch, but...nothing. And I couldn't find out from anyone where I could contact you. I even asked Rolfe, cooked up a story about how I'd promised you some book or other, and he said to give it to him and he'd forward it. The bastard was as smooth as butter.'

Capri bit her tongue. No use defending Rolfe at this point. She looked away to where the waves thundered regularly onto the shore below them. 'Go on.'

'When I learned you'd been in that accident I was frantic. Rolfe was already gone by the time I heard, and I was still trying to find out where you were and if you'd been badly hurt when I saw you walking along the beach...I've never been so relieved in my life.'

He had cared for her, she supposed, and with a flash of compunction she said, 'I'm sorry you were worried.'

'Well, the main thing is you're okay. Except for this memory loss. I wish I could help.'

'Thank you.' He sounded sincere, and his eyes were

anxious. She moistened her lips. 'Did...did I tell you why I was unhappy with Rolfe?'

Gabriel shrugged. 'He's wedded to his business, and his wife came second. And he wanted children, while you...' He shook his head.

'I didn't?' Capri asked, astonished.

'You insisted on my using protection even though you were on the pill. You were terrified of getting pregnant.'

'To *you*, maybe!' She certainly wouldn't have wanted a child that wasn't her husband's. And there were other reasons for caution, anyway.

'You didn't want to have Rolfe's baby either.'

'Did I tell you that?'

Gabriel shrugged. 'You made it obvious. I guess he wanted to tie you down, stop you straying.'

'Rolfe isn't like that.'

He looked derisive. 'He's exactly the type. To that kind of man a family is proof of his virility, another status symbol like his car and this house.'

'*You* have a nice house,' she said pointedly.

Gabriel grinned, apparently not offended. 'So I do. But Rolfe didn't always have money. Men like that— who've made a fortune on their own, and so early in life—they're driven. Obsessive compulsives who have to keep proving themselves, always looking out for something bigger, better, faster—prettier.' He cast Capri a shrewd glance. 'I admire Rolfe in lots of ways. But you have to understand—he's never going to be satisfied with what he has. He'll always be reaching for something else.'

'I doubt if you know him well enough to dissect him,' Capri said coldly.

'I know his type,' Gabriel insisted. 'I'm sure he despises me because I have enough money to pursue the small talent I have and make the most of it.' Ignoring the quick upward flick of her eyelashes at this accurate summing up, he went on, 'But the fact is, I can offer a woman the kind of security he never will, no matter how much money he makes. Because I have nothing to prove.'

Rolfe had said she was insecure. Gabriel had an uncanny ability to probe sore spots. She steered him away from the uncomfortable subject. 'What about your painting? Don't you want to prove yourself there?'

'I know I'm good, but no genius, and I don't have an overwhelming ambition.'

'Perhaps you'd paint better if you did.'

'Or perhaps I'd just drive myself and everyone around me nuts trying to achieve the impossible. I'm happy the way I am.' Gabriel's voice changed, lowered. 'And I've never been as happy as I was in those few weeks when you and I were together.' His eyes sought and held hers, and she stirred uncomfortably.

Shaking her head, she said, 'Gabriel…whatever might have been between us, it's over. It should never have happened.'

He leaned forward and grasped her hands in his. 'You can't say that! You don't even remember how we were together! It was…incandescent, darling! If you'd just give me the chance I could show you—'

Her hands trembled in his as she tried to withdraw them. 'Please, Gabriel—'

'Capri! Darling, listen to me—'

'Good afternoon,' Rolfe's deep, decisive voice interrupted.

Capri gasped, finally pulling her hands away from Gabriel's slackened grasp. 'Rolfe! I didn't hear the car.'

'You don't from this side of the house,' he told her.

He was carrying a florist's bouquet, wrapped in stiff green paper and tied with a red ribbon. 'Hello, Gabriel.'

Gabriel stood up, trying to look nonchalant. 'Hi.'

'You're leaving?' Rolfe suggested politely, in a voice like tempered steel.

Gabriel glanced at Capri, and she said, 'Yes. He was just going. Gabriel has been...trying to help me remember...'

'Really.' The steel was still there. His eyes seared her. 'Any luck?'

Capri shook her head. There seemed to be an obstruction in her throat, and for the life of her she couldn't say any more.

'Pity,' Rolfe said. 'Well...' turning to the other man '...thanks for trying.'

It was a dismissal, and Gabriel weathered it as best he could, with a sickly smile and a shrug. 'I'll see you again,' he offered, looking at Capri.

She didn't answer.

Rolfe waited until Gabriel had loped down the slope and disappeared along the beach. Then he tossed the bouquet onto the table in front of Capri, making her flinch. 'I bought those for you,' he said. 'I'm going to have a shower.'

She sat staring at the flowers while he went inside, nausea curling in her stomach, an anxious pulse fluttering in her throat. There were carnations, small furled pink lilies, a few tight rosebuds, and some blue flowers she couldn't identify. It was an expensive bouquet.

After a while she picked it up with shaking fingers and carried it inside.

In the utility room she found a plain pottery vase and filled it with water. Arranging the flowers would give her something to do.

Fiercely concentrating, she was picking up the last carnation when she sensed Rolfe's shadowy presence in the doorway, and forced herself to turn a calm face to her husband.

Her hands had stopped shaking, and her voice was steady, if a trifle lower than usual. 'They're lovely flowers,' she said. 'Thank you.'

He'd changed into jeans with a loose shirt. His hair was damp, sleeked back from his forehead, and his eyes looked very dark. If his shower had been a cold one it hadn't improved his temper. He was keeping anger fiercely under control, but it emanated from him in waves. 'Do you want to tell me,' he said gratingly, 'why Gabriel Blake was holding your hands?'

No, I don't want to, was her first, involuntary thought. Standing in the doorway he looked big and implacable, and as if a wrong word would provoke some violent reaction. Capri swallowed, and turned to blindly poke the carnation into her arrangement. The stalk snapped in the middle, and she vented her feelings in a small exclamation.

Rolfe stepped forward until he was beside her, so close she could smell the soap he'd used in the shower. 'Capri?'

She looked down at the shortened carnation stalk, and decided on the coward's way out. 'Some people are like that,' she said. 'You know, they touch a lot.' She risked a fleeting glance up, saw a frown deepen between Rolfe's black brows. 'It doesn't mean anything. He's an artist,' she added hurriedly, tarring all artists with the same empathetic brush. 'He was trying to help.'

'Help you remember?'

'Yes.' Carefully this time, she tucked the carnation into the vase. 'If we'd been up to anything, Rolfe, we wouldn't have sat in full view of anyone strolling along the beach. Would we?'

She dared to turn then, clutching the counter behind her and looking with deliberately limpid eyes into his face. 'I don't even know the man,' she said truthfully. She'd only met him twice, and briefly, since returning. 'I remember nothing about him.'

'He knows you.'

We knew each other very well, Gabriel had said that first morning. Her heart shrank. 'So do you,' she said huskily. 'And you're my husband.'

His eyes searched hers, and she met them with an effort, willing him to believe that whatever had happened in the past, and whatever he had known or suspected, she meant to be a faithful wife from now on.

Rolfe moved, his hands on the counter trapping her between his strong arms. The perfume of the flowers floated about them. 'Yes.'

He leaned towards her, and his lips brushed the side of her neck, moving back and forth.

Her hands clutched hard at the wood behind her, and she closed her eyes. He wasn't touching her except with his mouth, but she could feel the heat of his body, only inches from hers, and the seductive aroma of his skin mingled with the flower scents and the clean smell of soap.

His mouth wandered to her ear, and his teeth nipped the lobe, drawing it between his lips. She choked in a breath, and Rolfe muttered something and moved closer, his hands raking into her hair. She felt the feathering of his breath against her eyelids, her cheek, before his lips parted hers in a devastating, ruthlessly sexual kiss. There was no gentleness there, none of the tender consideration he had shown her before.

Her hands left the counter and she grabbed at his shirt, then slid her arms about his neck, blindly hanging onto him as a tide of heat weakened her body. His warm, muscular thigh nudged hers apart, and she made a muffled sound of confused pleasure and alarm. One of his hands shifted, a thumb massaging the hollow at the base of her throat, increasing her heart's rhythm. And then his hand moved down again, inside the collar of her blouse, impatient with the buttons that impeded him, tearing them asunder so he could touch her, cup her breast in its lacy covering, slide around to release the catch of her bra and then find her breast again, naked and eager with its yearning centre.

His touch was rough but exciting, his mouth ever more demanding as he deepened the kiss to a white-hot intimacy. She was jammed up against the counter behind her, overwhelmed by his physicality, surrounded by him, all sensation suspended except those provided by him, all sound blocked out but his warm breath and her own blood pounding in her ears.

He pressed his thigh against her, and she drew a shuddering breath, the blood thrumming in her temples.

His hand circled her throat, the thumb pressing the shallow hollow, the hammering pulse, and she made a small sound in response, bewildered and not a little frightened by the overpowering sensations that weakened her knees and made her body seem weightless, her head dizzy.

And then suddenly he flung himself back, and her arms fell away from him, her hands grabbing at the counter to keep herself upright.

CHAPTER TEN

'NO—*DAMN*!' Rolfe's hand slapped on the counter alongside one of hers. His face darkly flushed, he shook his bent head. '*No,*' he said hoarsely. 'Not like this.'

Capri felt as if she'd been doused in cold water.

'I should have known better than to touch you,' he muttered, lifting his hand and running it over his still damp hair. 'Are you okay?'

'Yes.' Except for a crying need that he obviously had no intention of satisfying. Automatically she grasped at the edges of her ruined blouse and pulled it across her naked breasts, which still throbbed from his attentions. 'It's all right.'

'It's not all right! I behaved like an animal. A mindless, territorial animal. I swear it won't happen again.'

Then he was gone, striding out of the room and closing the door with a snap behind him.

Rolfe was very polite to her for the next couple of days. Capri felt as though he'd built a wall between them over which they exchanged meaningless pleasantries, like good neighbours who wanted to get along although they had little in common.

When he asked at lunchtime on Saturday, 'What time do you want to be at Thea and Ted's tonight?' she thought about making some excuse after all, sure she'd never felt less like socialising. But coping with a crowd might be easier than staying home in this suffocating atmosphere.

'Any time it suits you,' she answered.

'About six-thirty, then?' He might have noticed the flutter of a nervous pulse in her throat. 'If you've changed your mind we can still cancel.'

'I have to meet people some time, and...maybe something will happen.'

'Maybe.' He cast her an odd, brooding look. Her nervousness must be showing, because he added, 'I'll be right there.'

'Thank you, Rolfe. You're very good to me.'

He pushed his chair back and stood up, ready to go back to his office. 'I always wanted to be,' he said, 'if only you'd let me.'

The words woke a faint echo in her brain. Something Treena had said...about most people being nice if you just gave them a chance.

She dressed for the barbecue in black jeans and a silky green and black patterned blouse, with black wedge sandals on her feet.

When she walked into the living room where Rolfe, also wearing jeans, with a blue cambric shirt, was just taking a bottle of chilled white wine from the fridge, he turned and stared. 'I never have got over how lovely you are, Capri. You seem to grow more so every day.'

'Thank you.' She'd smudged olive-green eyeshadow over her lids, shaded it into a silver-grey one under her brows, used a kohl pencil and some mascara. And coloured her lips a bright candy-pink. It had occurred to her as she brushed blusher along her cheekbones that she was applying a mask of some sort—camouflage to make her feel more confident. 'Do we take food? I could make a quick salad.'

'Thea will have all that in hand. But there's an unopened round of Brie in here, if you feel you'd like to contribute.'

She took it, and a packet of crackers to go with it, presenting them to their hostess on their arrival while Rolfe handed over the wine.

Thea kissed them both and put the offerings down on a nearby table that had been set up on the lawn near a big gas-fired barbecue. 'Thanks, though you didn't need to. I do love your hair short, Capri. I didn't tell you the other day, did I? Oh, there's Nic and Sarah arriving. Do you remember them?'

Rolfe said, 'I do, of course.' He turned to greet them, sliding an arm about Capri's waist. 'Darling, Nic and Sarah Anderson live just down the road from us.' At their puzzled smiles, he said, 'Since the accident Capri's been suffering from amnesia.'

Sarah was a small, bouncy blonde. 'That must be so difficult.' Her face showed concern. 'I expect it will come right, though.'

Another couple joined them, who also expressed their commiseration. Soon there was a small circle around them, and someone asked, 'What did the doctors say?'

'That it's probably temporary,' Capri answered.

Rolfe cut in. 'We hope it will clear up naturally.'

Sarah nodded thoughtfully, her eyes curious but sympathetic.

'Capri—' Gabriel Blake joined the group, giving Capri an intense, penetrating look before he smiled at her. 'How are you? And...Rolfe.'

Rolfe said, 'Good evening, Gabriel. Will you excuse us? I'd like to find my wife somewhere to sit.'

The group parted with murmurs of, 'Of course,' and, 'There are chairs over there...' And Gabriel stepped aside. Capri could feel his eyes following them as Rolfe led her to a table where two other people already sat holding glasses.

Guests sprawled on the grass, occupied the folding chairs and tables their hosts had set out on the lawn and a wide deck, or stood about chatting, glasses in hand. Thea had said this wasn't a party, but there were twenty or so people present.

Several of them had commented on her hairstyle. She must have had it cut in Australia. She remembered that Rolfe had touched her hair in the hospital that first day after she'd woken, and said it suited her.

'Food's ready!' Ted called.

When Capri and Rolfe had filled two plates with steak, chops and salads their seats had been taken.

Rolfe looked about and led her to a rustic seat in the shadow of a spicy-scented pepper tree, away from the circle of light around the barbecue.

'How is it?' he asked her quietly after a while.

'The food, or the party—I mean the get-together?'

Rolfe smiled, the first genuine smile he'd given her since he'd found her with Gabriel days before. 'Both, I guess. Is it a bit much, meeting all these people again?'

'Everyone's very understanding. Although one or two,' she added wryly, 'have decided I'm mentally retarded.'

'Does it bother you?'

'Not much. I suppose that's one advantage. I don't know them any more, so what does their opinion matter?'

Rolfe laughed and touched her arm. 'Good thinking.' His hand stayed on her arm, absently roving over her skin. 'You don't remember anyone?'

'I'm afraid not.'

When they'd finished eating he took her plate. 'There's fruit salad and marshmallows.'

Capri shook her head. 'But don't let me stop you. I'll have a coffee when you're ready.'

He went off, slipping under the overhanging branches and making his way to the table.

Surely someone, something here should be familiar? She closed her eyes and listened to the laughter and voices, concentrating hard, trying to remember anything...

A hand gripped her shoulder from behind. She looked round, tipping her head, thinking Rolfe was back already.

'Gabriel!' Carefully she freed herself.

Tensely he asked, 'Are you okay? Rolfe didn't...do anything to you the other day?'

He kissed me. But she couldn't tell Gabriel that. 'Of course not. He isn't a monster.'

'Listen, darling—I don't know what Rolfe is playing at, but when you left him I could swear you didn't mean to come back.'

Capri stood up to face him across the bench. 'I don't believe that!'

Maybe she didn't sound too convincing, because even as she spoke she recalled Rolfe saying starkly, *And yet you left me.* He'd glossed over that afterwards, but an unequivocal denial wasn't possible as long as her memory remained inaccessible.

Gabriel's hand curled over the back of the seat. 'We'd talked about it...I wanted you to come to America with me.'

'Then why didn't I go? I must have decided to stay with my husband.'

'You needed time to think, you said, to plan. You

wanted me to wait, only I couldn't postpone the New York dates. The exhibition had been booked for months. And then, when I got back you'd gone. So you *didn't* stay with him, did you?'

Capri put a hand briefly to her forehead. 'Maybe I left both of you.' Very possibly she'd needed time alone to sort herself out. Finding her father might have just been an excuse to get away from both husband and lover, to decide who she really loved and what she should do about it.

'Come and see me,' Gabriel begged, 'next time Rolfe goes to the factory.'

'I can't,' she said steadily. 'I won't deceive my husband.'

'Until the next time…' Gabriel jeered, suddenly straightening, his expression becoming hard. 'And the next poor sucker who thinks you love him.'

Capri shook her head. 'There won't be a next time—'

'There will,' he asserted, his eyes shrewd and coldly assessing now. And cruel. 'I know your sort of woman, Capri. I should have recognised it earlier, only I was so besotted with you I couldn't see straight. No man can satisfy you—'

'You don't know what you're talking about!'

'Oh, yes, I do.' He leaned closer. 'You're looking for someone to replace the father who left you when you were a child. A daddy-figure. You'll go from man to man for the rest of your life and you won't be happy with any of them.' He made an angry, disgusted gesture. 'Because no one can live up to the idealised figure in your poor warped little mind. Not your stepfather, not your husband…and not your lovers. I could almost pity Rolfe—*he'll* never be able to hold you, either, not even with a wedding ring. I might have been the first lover you've had since you married him, but I won't be the last.'

'You're wrong.' She felt battered, as if he'd physically assaulted her—and afraid. Could his brutal assessment be correct? *Was* that why she had turned to him? Because Rolfe had been unable to satisfy some futile subconscious longing for her absent father? 'It's not true.'

But she didn't know if it was true or not. Gabriel liked dissecting people but that didn't mean he was always right. Although clever he was hardly unbiased.

'You need help,' he told her. His angry blue stare raked her. 'Has it occurred to you that Rolfe would just as soon you never recovered your memory?'

'Don't be silly!'

'It suits him that you've forgotten what went on in your marriage before.'

'Rolfe's been very supportive. He'll stand by me.'

Rolfe's hard voice cut in, making her start. 'I promise you I will, darling, though I'm not sure in what connection?' His arm curved about her, his fingers firm on her waist. In his other hand he held a bowl of fruit salad topped with marshmallows and a scoop of ice cream.

Before she could frame an answer Gabriel said rather loudly, 'I was just saying that if Capri were my wife I'd want to get to the bottom of this amnesia thing as soon as possible.'

Rolfe's fingers bit into her side. 'Capri's not your wife,' he said evenly, 'she's mine.'

'I heard you earlier tonight,' Gabriel flung at Rolfe. 'You hope it will clear up naturally,' he sneered. 'Has she seen a specialist since she got home?'

'I saw a neurologist in the hospital,' Capri said. 'And

if I want another opinion it isn't Rolfe's decision, it's mine.'

Rolfe added, 'And she'll make it without any help from...outsiders.'

'*Capri*—' There was pleading in Gabriel's voice, and she couldn't help a wrenching sense of compassion.

But she felt also a sick fear of what he might say. 'I know you're trying to help, Gabriel,' she said quickly. 'I realise we've been...you've been my friend in the past. But *I don't remember you*. And...what I do with my life is none of your concern.'

'I think that about sums it up,' Rolfe said. 'Come on, Capri, time we went back to the others.'

He turned her and shifted his hand to her shoulder, the fingers gripping.

'It's all right,' she murmured. 'I'm not going to run away.'

'What?' They came into the light and his eyes seemed glazed as he looked down at her.

'You're bruising my shoulder.'

He eased his hold, rubbing at the spot instead. 'I didn't realise.' His face was both grim and remote. He still carried the bowl, but as they neared the table he reached over and put it down.

'Don't you want it after all?' Capri enquired.

'I'm not hungry any more.' He stopped walking and let his hand slide from her arm. 'What was that about?'

Her gaze faltered at the dark, almost hostile glint in his eyes. 'He's...concerned about me. Lots of people tonight have asked questions, given us advice.'

'I'm concerned about you too, Capri.' He faced her and took both her hands in his.

Capri chewed momentarily on her lower lip. 'I really

expected that once I was home everything would come back to me.'

Rolfe was silent for several seconds. When he spoke again his voice was low and rasping. 'I'll take you to see someone.'

'You'd come with me?'

'Certainly.' His voice sounded clipped.

'Can you spare the time from your work?'

She was puzzled by the narrowed, searching look he gave her. 'I'll make the time somehow,' he answered at last. 'If anything can bring back your memory, I want to be there when it happens.'

She smiled at him, and saw his eyes darken further, his gaze slipping to her mouth.

The smile faded from her lips and a pulse started to beat heavily in her throat. Involuntarily she lifted her head further, tipped her face to him.

The bouncy blonde, Sarah, swooped on them, waving a frankfurter in a long bun. 'Break it up, you two,' she teased. 'You're heating up the air worse than the barby.' Dramatically she fanned her face with her free hand. 'I suppose it's like a second honeymoon.' She grinned. 'Seeing you can't remember the first one, Capri?'

Nic, as tall and gangly as Sarah was small and rounded, came up behind her and laid his hands on his wife's shoulders. 'Sarah's never won any prizes for tact,' he told Capri. He dropped a kiss on the blonde curls resting against his chest. 'But I love her anyway.'

Capri could see that he did, and the smile Sarah slanted up at him made it clear the sentiment was returned.

Rolfe released Capri's hands and hung a casual arm about her shoulders. 'Jealousy will get you nowhere,' he drawled, making Sarah laugh.

'You two must come round to our place one evening,' she said. 'There won't be such a crowd for Capri to cope with.' Her sympathetic glance told Capri she'd noticed signs of strain. 'We'll have a nice quiet dinner.'

'She can cook,' Nic told Capri proudly.

'Yeah, that's why the brute married me.'

'Why else?' Nic grinned. 'Plus I've always been partial to blondes with curves in the right places.'

His hands wandered and Sarah slapped them away. 'Hey, wait till we get home! I've just been telling these two off for that kind of thing.'

Nic leered down at her. 'Can we go home now?'

'No, you big oaf! I haven't had my dessert yet.' Sarah rolled her eyes. 'Men!' she said to Capri. 'You wonder how they even *think* they can run the world when they have such trouble getting their minds to climb higher than their belt-buckles.'

Her expression, as much as the words, forced a laugh from Capri, and she felt Rolfe relax beside her as Nic said, 'I resent that. Mine frequently climbs as high as my stomach—which, let me remind you, is above the belt.'

'Nic's a doctor, Capri,' Rolfe told her. 'So he should know.'

Capri smiled. 'What do you do?' she asked Sarah.

Her husband answered, 'For my sins, she's my partner in local practice. Likes to keep an eye on me.' He waggled his eyebrows at his wife as she made a face at him.

When they'd wandered off, amicably arguing, Capri looked after them enviously. They were so at ease with each other, confident in their mutual love. 'Are they good friends of ours?' she asked Rolfe.

'We bump into each other at affairs like this. They invited us for dinner when we first arrived here.

And…Sarah attended you when you had the miscarriage. She's not your regular doctor—you prefer to see a man in Auckland—but it was an emergency and Sarah was closer.'

'I like her. She's not pretending that nothing's wrong with me—she even teased us about it. But she doesn't make me feel like some kind of freak or someone who needs to be humoured.'

'Do *I* do that?' Rolfe asked, looking down at her.

'No! But a few people tonight…'

'Would you like to go home?' he asked abruptly. 'If you've had enough we can leave any time.'

She looked about them. Thea caught her eye and came over to them. 'I've hardly had a chance to talk to you two! Are you having a good time?'

Capri assured her that they were. 'But I'm a bit tired. I guess I haven't got over the accident properly yet. Rolfe was just offering to take me home.'

'Oh, that's a shame. Give me a ring some time, Capri. We'll have lunch—a girls' day out.'

'I'd like to do that. It was a great—um—barbecue.'

'Oh, we know how to party, don't we, girl?' Thea executed a little dance step and then stopped, looking guilty. 'Damn, I forgot! Sorry. It's so…peculiar!' She grimaced.

Capri smiled. 'It's pretty strange for me too.'

After they'd said their goodnights Rolfe ushered her to the car. The journey home was accomplished in minutes, and she wondered why he'd bothered to drive them. They could easily have walked.

Inside the house Capri slipped off her shoes and, swinging them in her hand, turned to see Rolfe regarding her with a slightly amused smile.

'What?' she queried.

'Just that habit you have of taking your shoes off after a party. Of course you will wear those ridiculous heels...'

'These aren't all that ridiculous.' She glanced down at them. 'I've never liked wearing shoes. My mother used to be forever telling me to pick them...up...' Her voice trailed away.

She stood looking at him, jolted back to awareness of where she was, what she'd said. But even as she tried to grasp and retain the memory, the faint echo of a long-ago voice, a place, vanished into the recesses of her mind.

'You remember?' he asked alertly.

She sighed. 'Not really. Just for a second there was something, but it's gone now.'

They stood looking at each other and Capri felt suddenly awkward. Rolfe hadn't kissed her goodnight since the episode in the utility room. Had barely touched her until tonight, when he'd had an arm about her waist or shoulders practically all the time. 'Thank you for taking me to the barbecue,' she said politely. 'It was good for me.'

'I'm glad you enjoyed yourself.'

Possibly too strong a term, but the short respite among other people—and maybe the moderate amount of alcohol they'd had—seemed to have eased the atmosphere, despite the unsettling interlude with Gabriel Blake.

She wondered if that was something they should talk about, bring out in the open.

'About Gabriel...' she started tentatively.

His face closed. 'I think it's best if we don't discuss him, Capri.'

It was an easy way out, but she wasn't sure if that

was best. Feeling her way, she asked, 'Why do you think that?'

A disturbing glitter returned to Rolfe's eyes. 'What has he been saying to you?'

Capri swallowed. Rolfe wasn't stupid...if he didn't know or have some suspicion about the affair that Gabriel insisted she'd been having, he couldn't be totally unaware of Gabriel's interest in her. 'He...he says he loves me.'

Rolfe's teeth showed in what was hardly a smile. 'And do you love him?'

'No!' Vehemently, she shook her head. 'I don't even know him any more! And if I did—I'm married to *you*, Rolfe!'

'Yes.' His teeth snapped together. Then he moved, catching her chin in the cup of his big hand. 'So,' he enquired softly, his eyes compelling her to answer, 'do you love *me*, Capri?'

CHAPTER ELEVEN

HE LOOKED dangerous, his face taut and fierce.

Capri's heart thudded with primordial fear, and with something that wasn't fear at all, something hot and hungry and alien. The same bewildering mixture of emotions that she always experienced when he touched her in any remotely sexual way. She wanted him on a deep, wholly instinctive level. That much she couldn't deny. But was that love?

Forcing herself not to flinch from his demanding gaze, she swallowed once. 'I don't know.'

Rolfe didn't move and his expression didn't alter, only the faintest flicker of his dark lashes showing any hint of reaction.

'If I didn't love you,' she rationalised, 'I wouldn't have married you. But I don't remember...'

'All right.' He released her and shoved both hands into his belt. 'Tell me how you do feel about me.'

Her fingers tightened their grip on her shoes. 'I think you're very...attractive. And you've been remarkably thoughtful and understanding.'

He made a small, derisory sound, but didn't take his hard stare from her. 'I said, how do you *feel*?'

'Feel?' Her eyes momentarily glazed as she thought about it. 'I feel...confused.' Her face warming, she said honestly, 'When you kiss me...touch me...I want to reciprocate, but at the same time I'm...nervous.'

'I frightened you the other day.'

'A bit.'

'And yet you responded, even though I was rough,' he reminded her harshly.

She couldn't meet his eyes now. 'I know I did. But I could sense that you were angry.' She took an unsteady breath. 'That's why you stopped, isn't it?'

She lifted her eyes then, and saw the way his jaw clenched.

'Yes,' he said. 'That's why I stopped. In that mood I should have kept my hands off you.'

She ventured a shaky smile. 'I don't believe you'd ever hurt me, Rolfe. You're not that kind of man.'

His expression changed so suddenly it was almost as though she'd hit him—he was clearly rocked by her confident statement. Then he said, with an edge of mockery, 'But that's the point, of course. You don't know what kind of man I really am. Do you?'

That *was* the point. While her instinct and the little she knew of him told her he was a man of integrity, a man she could trust, she was acutely aware of his own complex feelings simmering under the surface of the restrained, considerate manner. Of desire dangerously mixed with fiercely leashed rage. 'I'm learning,' she assured him. 'There's still a lot I have to learn about myself, as well.'

His grave expression softened into a weary, slightly cynical resignation. 'I'm learning about you too—this new you. It's something of a revelation to me, especially this almost virginal reticence about sex.'

Capri's teeth caught her lower lip. 'I can't help it…I'm sorry.'

He nodded. 'I don't mean to rush you. This isn't easy for either of us. You're tired.'

'Yes.' She hesitated a moment longer, then stepped

forward and reached up to brush her lips against his cheek. 'Goodnight, Rolfe.'

She was about to move away when his hands caught her shoulders, his fingers biting into her flesh. 'Damn!' he breathed, his eyes burning. And as she blinked up at him his voice roughened. 'You always did like to play with fire. Is that what the thing with Gabriel Blake was about? Was it meant to force some kind of reaction from me?'

Her eyes widened in shock. 'No!' And then, honestly, 'I don't know...I don't *remember*! You know that!'

The blaze died, but it was replaced by a cold, even deadlier doubt. 'Do I?' He gave her a narrow, laser-like stare. 'Or is this all some elaborate con-job to get you out of trouble?'

'No!' Once before he'd suggested something of the sort—but had seemed to immediately reject it. Did he still suspect she was faking, after all?

'I warn you,' he said slowly, 'if you're stringing me along you'll have reason to be afraid.'

'I'm not!' Capri balled her fists and thrust at his chest, with no effect. 'Let me go!' Panic and anger made her voice an octave higher.

He did, leaving her standing with her arms instinctively wrapped across her breasts.

Relieved, but furious herself now, she said, 'I'm not making any of this up! And I don't know why you should think...suspect...that I'm pretending to have lost my memory.' To her dismay her voice wobbled.

She saw him close his eyes before he lifted a hand and kneaded his temples. 'I apologise,' he said. 'Even if that were so, I shouldn't have mauled you. That was unconscionable.'

'I'm not hurt. You haven't done any damage.'

He dropped his hand and stared at her. She could see she'd surprised him again. 'Go to bed, Capri,' he said. 'Tomorrow we'll talk about getting you some professional help.'

'Maybe we should both have some.'

'What?'

'Maybe we should have marriage counselling.'

He was silent for several long seconds. Then he said, 'That might not be a bad idea, but it's surely a bit pointless at this stage. I think counsellors need to hear both sides of the story, and you can't remember yours. We'd better work on the immediate problem first.'

At mid-morning Capri phoned Thea to thank her again for the barbecue and ask if she needed help to clean up.

Thea laughed. 'Heavens, no! I have a cleaner for that. It's practically all done. But listen, why don't you come over for lunch on the leftovers, and we'll have a coze? You can tell me all about this amnesia thing. It's just like a soap opera!'

'There isn't much to tell,' Capri protested mildly. 'But thanks,' she added. 'I'd like to come to lunch.' Thea might help fill some of the gaps in Capri's knowledge of herself and her former life.

Only Thea seemed more interested in the details of Capri's memory loss, and apparently she too was inclined to disbelieve in its reality. 'You're not having us all on?' she queried suspiciously, heaping salads onto her plate. 'Help yourself. There's plenty here.'

Capri took some salad too, and split a bread roll. 'I'm not having anyone on.' Why did those who seemed closest to her think she'd indulge in such an elaborate deception?

'You don't remember *anything*?'

'I remember practically nothing before I woke up in the hospital.'

'That's weird!' Thea forked up some lettuce. 'So what did you say to Gabriel?'

Capri spooned a mound of egg salad onto her plate. 'Gabriel?' she repeated cautiously.

'I saw him talking to you last night—and Rolfe barging in on it.'

'Rolfe didn't barge in.' Instinctively Capri defended him. But after all, this was one reason she'd accepted Thea's invitation. 'Why should Gabriel be upset?' she asked, hoping the question sounded innocent.

'Why?' Thea laughed. 'Girl, the man's madly in love with you! Has been for months.'

'Who told you that?' Capri raised a dread-laden gaze.

Thea rolled her eyes. 'I'm your best friend! D'you think I wouldn't know?'

Her voice low, Capri asked, 'Did I mention him to you?'

'Of course, honey. You laughed about it at first, but I could tell you were excited.'

'But Rolfe is my husband. So I wouldn't have...have let him down, would I?'

Thea raised her brows expressively, and laughed again. 'No?'

'Did I tell you I was having an affair with Gabriel?' Capri asked baldly.

'Not directly, but it didn't take a genius to figure it out. Besides, Gabriel isn't exactly discreet, you know. And you didn't seem to care particularly. You were spending your afternoons at his place while Rolfe was at work. All the neighbours must have known.'

'That doesn't necessarily mean...anything.'

'Oh, sure. Do you expect me to believe you were having afternoon tea?'

Capri looked at the food on her plate. She'd lost her appetite completely. Despite the warm day she felt cold. Forcing herself to look up, she asked the question that had burned in her mind for days. 'Do you think Rolfe knew?'

Thea chewed on a mouthful of salad. 'He's no fool. On the other hand, people *like* Rolfe. Maybe they would have covered up for his sake. I guess if no one told him—' she shrugged '—and if he trusted you...'

Capri flinched. Had he trusted her, and had she wantonly destroyed that trust? Was that where the underlying anger she sensed in him had come from?

'Mind you,' Thea decided, 'I wouldn't like your chances if Rolfe found out.'

Capri's lips pressed together. 'Rolfe would never be violent.'

'Not physically, no. But I don't think he'd stand for being cheated on either, if he knew...' Thea looked shrewdly pensive. 'He'd never let you get away with it. So I guess he didn't know about it, and you don't have a thing to worry about.'

Capri couldn't help an incredulous little laugh. 'I don't?'

'Here.' Thea grabbed a bottle of wine and poured some into the tall glass in front of Capri. 'You look as though you need this. Is Rolfe being difficult?'

Capri picked up the glass with an unsteady hand and took a cool sip. 'Rolfe's being wonderful. Gabriel was difficult. But I have to put my marriage first.'

'Well...if you say so.' Thea was clearly astonished. 'You were pretty keen on Gabriel.' She picked up her glass. 'Here's to a new start, if that's what you really want.'

It *was* what she wanted, passionately. To make up to Rolfe for whatever pain and injustice she might have inflicted on him in the blank, unremembered past.

The following week Capri and Rolfe had dinner with Sarah and Nic Anderson, and over drinks and food both of them showed a professional interest in Capri's medical history. 'Do you remember anything at all?' Nic questioned.

'I remember some ordinary, everyday things,' she told them. 'But almost nothing about my personal life.'

Nic said, 'Hmm, that type of amnesia is usually associated with some kind of emotional trauma, even when there's an immediate physical cause.'

Sarah nodded. 'The crash must have been pretty horrific. You'd have been scared out of your mind, very likely in pain before you blacked out, and possibly you'd seen things that you found too horrible to accept.'

'Understandable,' Nic decided, 'the old brain blocking out what it prefers not to remember.'

'So, it just decided not to,' Sarah concluded, 'and went a bit overboard, to make quite sure you didn't recall the nasty bits. At least until you were ready to deal with them.'

'Practically all my life,' Capri said wryly. 'It does seem a bit excessive.'

Rolfe looked from Capri to Sarah. 'So you agree that when she's strong enough her memory will return of its own accord?'

Nic and Sarah exchanged a professional glance. 'It's only a theory,' Sarah cautioned. 'Not a diagnosis. I've been reading up on the subject a bit since I heard—I hope you don't mind, Capri? But it's not our field really.'

'I don't mind.'

'This is mainly anecdotal,' Sarah told her, 'but for what it's worth, some people have spontaneously recovered from trauma-induced amnesia after another trauma. Not that I'd wish that on you.'

'We're not neurologists or psychiatrists,' Nic warned. 'You really need a specialist opinion.'

The talk turned to other things, and Capri found she was enjoying herself more than she could ever remember. She thought Rolfe was relaxed too, laughing aloud with Nic, and teasing Sarah.

At the end of the evening Rolfe tucked Capri into the car and drove them home.

He'd scarcely touched her since the night of Thea and Ted's barbecue, when she'd given him that inoffensive kiss on his cheek and he'd accused her of liking to play with fire. And she hadn't dared offer him any kind of caress after that. But tonight when they entered the house he kissed her cheek as they said goodnight, and she smelled the clean scent of him, mingled with the coffee they'd had before leaving, felt the warmth emanating from his body, and had to check an impulse to move closer and cuddle up to him.

Instead she went off to her own room and her lonely double bed.

A few days later Capri phoned Treena, and after answering the usual queries about her memory loss asked, 'Has Venetia started on the film yet?'

That was enough to divert Treena from the subject of Capri's health. She heard all about the director, the budget, the stars who were taking the lead roles, and of course Venetia's part, and hoped she was making the right fascinated noises.

'And she does *appreciate* you taking an interest, Capri!' Treena wound up finally. 'You know, she really was quite *thrilled* that you sent your congratulations.'

'I gather I've not always been very nice to my sister?'

'Oh, well…' Treena said vaguely. 'Sibling rivalry, I suppose. You were such an awkward teenager—and left home *far* too young but *I* couldn't stop you. You said Steve and I were holding you back, and accused us of favouring Venetia. Well, *that* was hardly new—ever since Venetia was born you'd been convinced that she *always* got a better deal—I guess it was something to do with the fact you were adopted!'

The room seemed to shift around her, then it steadied. 'I was adopted.' Yes. Of course.

Treena said defensively, 'It's no secret. You've always *known*.'

Capri gripped the receiver in her hand, her mind busy rearranging this knowledge of herself. 'What about Venetia?'

Treena's reply sounded almost sulky. 'Your father and I had been married ten *years* and it looked like we'd *never* have a baby, so we adopted you. A few years later Venetia came along. It didn't mean we didn't still love *you*. But she was premature and she needed a lot of care even after we brought her home.'

'I was jealous of her?'

'All your *life* you've been jealous of her,' Treena wailed. 'I guess you felt rejected.'

'I'm sure I'm fond of my sister, really,' Capri assured her. Venetia had been a bridesmaid at her wedding, hadn't she? 'Do give her my love.'

* * *

When they were walking on the beach after dinner, she asked Rolfe, 'Did you know I was an adopted child?'

Rolfe glanced at her. 'Yes.' He bent and picked up a crooked stick lying on the sand, then tossed it at the waves rolling in to shore before turning to her again. 'Your mother told you?'

'She mentioned it today.'

'Does it bother you?' His eyes were dark and watchful.

'No. It was a surprise at first, but then my life is full of surprises...' She gave a wry little smile. 'She says I was terribly jealous of my sister. Apparently I never seemed to believe that I was as much loved as Venetia.'

'Your mother cares a great deal about you. She was almost hysterical when I phoned her after the accident.'

Capri smiled faintly. 'She does tend to overreact.'

She wondered if Venetia had inherited her mother's temperament, while her own presumably owed more to her biological parents. 'Do you know who my natural parents are?' she asked. 'Did I know?'

'No.' His answer seemed abrupt. 'I wouldn't worry about it. You've enough to contend with for now.' He thrust his hands into his pockets, and walked on.

Capri fell into step alongside. 'I talked to Sarah today and she's agreed to be my doctor. It seems more sensible than having some man over an hour's drive away. I need to get my records for her. Do you have my present GP's address or phone number?'

'I'll find them for you. Sarah seems a good choice.'

'I thought I might make an appointment soon and take that letter they gave me at the hospital.'

He shot her a glance, his mouth momentarily compressing. 'I'll come with you.'

'I don't need you to hold my hand.'

'I don't mind. You may need me.'

Capri shook her head. She had become so reliant on him, almost shamefully so. Someday she had to start doing things for herself—by herself.

He searched her face as though he might press the issue, but before he could say more she said firmly, 'Honestly, I'll be fine on my own, Rolfe.'

'You might ask her,' he said unexpectedly, 'if it's normal to experience a personality change after a concussion.'

'Personality change?'

He gave her a rather odd smile. 'I'm not complaining, you understand, but...sometimes I can't believe you're the same woman I married.'

'Doesn't everyone change over time? I was rather young when we married.'

'Yes, you were...in years,' he acknowledged. 'I should have realised it.'

'But you didn't?'

'You had such an aura of sophistication,' he said frankly. 'When we first met I thought you were older. After I found out your age I felt a bit guilty, but you laughed and called me sweet and old-fashioned. You'd lived and worked in a world where I gather people grow up fast or go under.'

'Did you ask me to give up modelling when we got married?'

'That was your decision. I think you rather fancied being a kept woman for a while.' He smiled. 'In fact you were delightfully frank about enjoying that luxury.'

'Was I very good at modelling?'

'You weren't in the supermodel class. It was pretty much hand-to-mouth, with no guarantee of a steady income, although when you did get work the money was good. I guess you enjoyed the pace and the parties, and the occasional lucky break when you were handsomely paid for a few days' work. But it's very competitive and I don't think you had many regrets about giving it up.'

'Am I lazy, Rolfe?'

'I never meant to suggest that. You didn't have the fierce will to forge your way to the top that I suspect drives a lot of people in that type of business. I think you were ready to move on, and not quite sure what you wanted to do with your life.'

'How serious was I about designing?'

He shrugged. 'You were dead keen at first. But the market is hard to break into. It was disheartening.'

And he'd said she didn't turn out work consistently as the market expected. 'I suppose I needed something to do with my time.' Gabriel had said Rolfe was wedded to his work, implying that she'd been neglected. 'You were very involved with your business, I gather.' Too involved to spend as much time with his wife as she might have hoped, perhaps.

'You never minded enjoying the fruits of my labour,' he said dryly.

Capri sent him a straight look. 'Is this an old argument between us? Did I accuse you of deserting me for your work?'

His pained smile indicated she'd hit the mark. 'You were probably right. I was accustomed to throwing all my energies into the business. There's always some new problem to be solved—the need to maintain an edge over competitors, keep up with new technologies, fend off possible hostile takeovers. Maybe I never did give enough time to my marriage.' He threw her an apologetic look, and his voice lowered. 'When I saw you in the hospital, looking so bruised and fragile, believe me my conscience was working overtime. I should have just taken the time to be with you, *before* the accident made it imperative. I should have been with you on that train.'

'Don't beat yourself up over it,' Capri advised. 'You did what you believed was right. And I could have waited, as you asked. It wouldn't have killed me.' Rushing away without him had nearly killed her, she reflected. If he'd flown to Australia with her, would she have been on that train at all?

'I have been trying to delegate more,' Rolfe said. 'Recently I hired a personal assistant.'

'I don't know much about your business.'

'It's highly technical. You've never been interested.'

'Haven't I?' She'd loved him, and yet not been at all curious about what he did every day?

'Anyway,' he added, 'a lot of it's commercially sensitive. I can't tell you much.'

Later that evening when she said she was tired and got up to leave the lounge, Rolfe rose too and kissed her cheek as he often did, but tonight his mouth wandered to hers and stayed for a long, sweet, breathtaking moment.

Then he stepped back, his eyelids sweeping down as his chest rose and then fell. 'You'd better get off to bed,' he told her. 'Unless you'd like to come to mine?'

'I...not yet.' The words came out before she'd thought about them. She looked at him with trepidation, silently begging his understanding, patience. Perhaps she wouldn't feel ready until she could remember the former life that had slipped from her mind.

His mouth twisted. 'That's what I thought you'd say. There's no hurry, Capri. I'll see you in the morning.'

*   *   *

Capri's medical records arrived and Sarah's receptionist phoned to make an appointment for her.

When she told Rolfe he said, 'Are you sure you don't want me there?'

'No, really. I'm quite comfortable with Sarah, and you don't need to coddle me.' She hoped her refusal didn't make him feel rejected. 'And I need to learn not to lean on you so much.'

His frown was almost sceptical. 'Lean on me as much as you need to,' he invited, a smile replacing the frown. 'If you change your mind, I'll make sure I'm available that day.'

Capri shook her head. 'There's no need, honestly.'

When she kept the appointment Sarah asked some questions, read the letter Capri handed over and said, 'The first step is to get you to another specialist. There'll be a wait, I'm afraid, and he may want to order more tests before deciding where to go from there.'

When Capri told Rolfe he just nodded. 'Fine,' he said easily. 'But when you see this specialist, I'm definitely coming along.'

This time she didn't argue with him.

Living in the same house, there were inevitable intimacies. Capri knew Rolfe liked to use a particular soap in the shower, and what colour his toothbrush was. She even knew what kind of underwear he wore, and that he never bothered with a pyjama top. His suits were expensive and he had several, but at home he preferred jeans and T-shirts, or comfortable cotton trousers with casual shirts.

He swam several times a week even though the water was still cool, tempting only the hardiest swimmers. Neat and ordered in his office, he scattered clothing,

books and papers that he was working on about his bedroom, but tidied them up on the mornings when Hallie
was due to arrive.

His taste in music sometimes coincided with hers, but
he preferred the classics when he was tired. And she
sensed he'd had a particularly stressful day at the factory
when he took off his tie before he'd even entered the
house, walking in with it in one hand, his briefcase
swinging from the other.

He liked his coffee very hot, and his toast almost
burnt, with plenty of butter and a thick layer of mar-
malade. And he scraped the butter in the dish from the
top until it was concave, while she always took a sliver
from the end. He appreciated good wines, but after a
hard day's work was just as likely to pour himself a cold
beer.

He would turn on the television to watch a documen-
tary but hardly ever for drama or comedy. Yet he had a
strong, if understated, sense of humour and frequently
made her laugh.

And he liked to watch her, following her movements
with veiled attention, making her conscious of her body
and how she used it, and when she looked at him he'd
smile, his eyes dark and gleaming. Occasionally he
looked at her strangely, as if he found her deeply puzzling.

One evening when Capri was finishing a pastel drawing of wind-bent pingao grass growing by a driftwood
log, he asked to see her expanding portfolio of nature
pictures. 'You should get someone to look at these,' he
suggested. 'I think you've discovered a talent you may
not have known you had.'

Once she ventured to join him as he swam. It was late
afternoon and the sea looked balmy, silver lights glinting

from the sun. She saw Rolfe heading down to the water, and on impulse searched the drawers in her room until she found a thin electric-blue one-piece swimsuit. Other people had been swimming that afternoon as she sketched on the shore, but although the days were lengthening, summer hadn't really set in yet and the few times over the past weeks when she'd dipped her toes in, the water had been too cold to tempt her.

Braving the initial chill, she struck out from the shore with determination.

Rolfe saw her and waited, treading water as she breast-stroked out to him.

'Hi,' he said. 'This is a nice surprise.'

'I'm beginning to think it's not such a good idea. Why do you do it?'

'It's good exercise,' he said. 'And it beats cold showers.'

'Brr,' she gasped, moving her arms and legs to stay afloat and ward off the chill. 'Who needs cold showers?'

'*I* have, lately,' Rolfe told her grimly.

Despite the cold water she felt her body grow warm all over, and ducked her head, going into a shallow dive to come up some distance away. She shook her wet hair out of her eyes and rolled onto her back, floating. The sky was pale and almost clear, only a few ragged clouds hanging in the air.

'If you want to warm up you need to keep moving,' Rolfe said in her ear.

She hadn't realised he was so close. She turned over, and was slapped in the face by an incoming breaker.

Disoriented, she floundered, starting to sink before strong hands gripped her waist and Rolfe said, 'It's okay. Just relax.'

She gulped, tasting acrid salt, and coughed. 'I swallowed some.' She clutched at the wet skin of his shoulders, reassuringly solid and warm beneath the surface coolness.

His hands slipped about her, steadying her. 'You're okay,' he repeated.

'Thanks. I'm all right now.'

He didn't let her go, his legs moving against hers, buoying her up as his hand moved to her hips, bringing her closer. She felt his arousal against her thigh, and heat coursed through her, negating the chill of the water.

'Rolfe…?' she said uncertainly.

Another wave slapped over them, making her gasp.

'Sorry,' he said. 'You okay?'

'Yes.' Breathless, but all right.

He let her go then, but stayed nearby all the time, and when she said she was going in to shore he followed her.

He picked up their towels and wrapped one about her, hurrying her up the sand and inside the house. 'Have a warm shower,' he said. 'You're going blue.'

'What about you?' Her skin felt cold but tingly, invigorated. She took the towel from her shoulders and rubbed at her hair to stop it dripping on the carpet.

His gaze slid over her, and she realised that the form-fitting Lycra wasn't hiding a thing. 'Is that an invitation?'

'No!' Instinctively she backed, flushing all over.

He laughed, a little harshly. 'I'll use the other bathroom,' he said, and turned away.

CHAPTER TWELVE

WHEN the specialist appointment came round, Rolfe went along with her, and stayed while she was subjected to more tests. And the following week he travelled to Auckland with her again to hear the results.

'No physical abnormalities have been detected,' the doctor told them, her voice reassuringly calm. 'My best theory is that the concussion simply masked the real problem.'

'Real problem?' Rolfe was seated beside Capri, holding her hand. His grip tightened fractionally and he leaned forward, frowning.

'There's no sign of a physical cause. A psychiatrist may be able to help.' The specialist looked at Capri and then Rolfe as if anticipating an objection. But she had none, and Rolfe just sent her a searching look and said nothing. The doctor turned to her desktop computer. 'There may be a wait of several weeks.'

'Are you okay?' Rolfe asked her when they had returned to his car. His fingers on the key, he turned to survey her.

'A bit wrung out,' she admitted.

'We'd better get you something to eat,' he suggested. She'd been too anxious that morning to have anything but coffee and a half slice of toast.

The place he took her to was quiet and upmarket and obviously expensive. Rolfe ordered wine with their meal, and although he drank sparingly, the glass that he urged on her helped to relax her taut nerves.

He didn't seem in any hurry to leave, lingering over coffee after most of the lunchtime customers had left, while their waiter lurked discreetly in a corner of the room. 'How do you feel about seeing a psychiatrist?' he asked her.

Capri shrugged. 'I have a problem. Apparently a psychiatrist is the appropriate specialist. It doesn't bother you, does it?'

'Not at all. Do you want to go and browse some shops while we're here in Auckland? I know how much you love shopping.'

They went to Parnell, which Rolfe said was her favourite retail haunt. In a small woodware shop she took a fancy to a smooth, honey-coloured bowl with a lovely grain, made from recycled kauri timber, and Rolfe bought it for her.

Then they walked on to a fashion boutique where he stood patiently by while she inspected racks of clothing, but she left without purchasing anything. 'I've so many clothes already,' she explained. 'I don't know when I ever wore them all.'

'You managed.' He glanced at her. 'Does any of this seem familiar?'

'Only vaguely.' She looked around them. 'I wish...'

'Don't.' His finger eased the frown between her brows. 'Just let it ride for now. I shouldn't have raised the subject.' He slipped an arm about her waist and pulled her to his side.

They spent more time than they'd meant to browsing an art gallery and arguing the merits of the work on display. When they emerged the rush hour was in full roar, and Rolfe suggested, 'We could eat in the city before we go home.'

'We've already had one restaurant meal today. Could we get some takeaways back in Atianui?'

He looked at her curiously. 'If you like. I vote we have a drink or coffee and wait for the traffic to clear a bit before we get on our way, though.'

They found a pleasant garden bar, and while Capri had two glasses of dry white wine that he ordered for her, Rolfe drank one glass of beer and then switched to coffee. A bowl of mixed nuts had been set before them, and Capri began picking at them, idly popping them into her mouth.

'Now, that's typical.' Rolfe grinned.

Capri paused, a curved white nut in her hand.

'Picking out the cashews and leaving the rest.'

'Oh.' She hadn't realised she'd been doing that. 'Is it? They're my favourites.' But they were too expensive to have often...

'I know,' Rolfe said, dispelling the stray thought.

A musician set up his keyboard in a corner of the bar, and between the music and the talk all around there wasn't much chance for conversation. After a while Rolfe looked at his watch. 'We should be able to get out of the city without too much hassle now.'

Capri had trouble pulling her seat belt from its housing when they returned to the car, and Rolfe leaned across to do it for her, his breath fanning her hair away from her temples.

She turned her head a little. 'Thank you.'

His smile was tight as he straightened, and he didn't answer, but lifted his hand again and brushed his knuckles lightly over her cheek before turning to start the engine.

After he'd negotiated the Harbour Bridge and they were on their way north, she asked him, 'Rolfe, do I have any money of my own? I found a cheque book in my bag but there's no balance written in.' He'd given her what seemed a generous amount of housekeeping money in cash but she hadn't used it for her personal spending.

'You spent most of what you made while you were working, but you have a small personal account. Is there something you want money for?'

'Nothing in particular. But I'd like to know that I don't have to ask you if I do.'

'No need. You have credit cards on my accounts, and you've never been shy of using them. In fact I thought you rather enjoyed doing so.' At her surprised look, he said, 'We're not short of money, Capri.'

'I know that.' She'd known it since she first set foot in the house—a house where she'd lived for two years and yet still failed to feel at home. 'Were my parents not well off?' she asked.

The change of subject seemed to disconcert him. 'Your parents?'

'I suppose,' she said, thinking aloud, 'my mother must have struggled, bringing up two girls on her own after my father left.'

'I'm sure it wasn't easy.'

'I don't feel used to having plenty of money,' she explained. 'Perhaps it goes back to my childhood.'

'You're probably right,' he agreed.

Some time later they stopped outside the sole takeaway bar and restaurant at Atianui. Rolfe asked, 'Are you sure you want takeaways? We could see if the restaurant has a table free.'

'Would you prefer that?'

'I thought you might.'

Capri shook her head. 'I feel like junk food tonight. Chips and...'

'Crumbed oysters?' Rolfe supplied as she paused for thought. 'You don't like batter, or white fish unless it's raw in sushi.'

'Or in a salad,' she agreed. 'Thanks for remembering.'

He looked as though he would say something, but changed his mind, instead slanting her a smile before opening the car door to climb out.

When they reached the house Capri tipped the food onto two plates and took them to the terrace outside, along with knives and forks.

It was getting dark, but an outside light allowed them to see the food, and the wine that Rolfe had poured.

'Fish and chips and a good Riesling,' Capri commented. 'I suppose it's a bit of a contradiction.'

'I've always thought fish and chips is a noble meal when it's properly done. You're the one who's suspicious of junk food.'

'I suppose being in modelling makes one very conscious of diet. But I've never had a weight problem.'

Rolfe arched an eyebrow and she said uncertainly, 'Well...not that I can recall.'

It was fully dark when they had finished, and they emptied the bottle of wine, Rolfe declining her offer to make coffee.

A huge pumpkin moon hung over the darkened horizon, gilding a broad band of ripples all the way to shore. The air was still, and warm from the day's sun.

'Let's go for a walk,' Capri suggested. It was later than usual, but the moon cast a white glow almost as bright as daylight.

Rolfe shifted the empty glass in his hand, drawing silent circles on the table. 'A walk on the beach in the moonlight?' His eyes searched her face, then he abruptly stood up. 'All right. I guess I can take it.' He held out his hand.

'If you'd rather not…'

He reached over and snagged her wrist. 'Come on,' he said brusquely, 'before I think better of this.'

The sand was cool and white in the moon's glow, and Capri slipped off her shoes, leaving them at the edge of the lawn.

Rolfe bent to shed his shoes too, and rolled his trouser legs above his ankles. He'd already removed his tie, leaving it hanging over the back of his chair before they ate, and his sleeves were carelessly folded back.

Capri was wearing the simple green dress he'd bought her, her favourite, that somehow she felt more comfortable in than any of the lovely clothes in her wardrobe. Rolfe took her hand again, turning in the direction away from Gabriel Blake's house. Capri determinedly banished all thought of Gabriel.

The waves whispered along the sand in curving white lines, leaving gleaming smoothness behind. A faint breeze arose, fluttering Capri's skirt and smoothing Rolfe's hair away from his forehead, throwing the strong profile into relief against the moon's light.

Capri shivered a little, and she rubbed at gooseflesh with her free hand.

'You're cold?' Rolfe asked.

'Not really. Just the breeze is coolish.'

His arm came about her, drawing her close before they strolled on. His hand warmed her skin. Capri raised her own arm and draped it round his waist. She felt very comfortable.

One wave scudded white-foamed and fast, swinging inland further than the others, and caught their feet, making Capri gasp at the chill on her toes.

'You all right?'

'Yes.' She laughed. 'I wasn't expecting that.'

'The tide's on its way in.'

As they walked further, their feet sinking now into the wet sand, she asked, 'Did we ever swim at night?'

'Only after…' He paused, then went on deliberately, 'Only after we'd made love on the beach.'

He'd said they'd done that. 'Where was that?' she asked him. Most of the beach was lined with houses, and fairly open. She couldn't imagine she'd have been really happy about risking possible exposure.

'There's a grove of trees over there.' He pointed. 'Some have grown together and fused. With the branches overhanging, it makes a cosy little cave.'

'Oh, yes, I've seen it.'

'But it brought back no memories.'

'No. Perhaps if…'

He stopped walking, and drew her into his arms. 'If…?' he repeated, his breath stirring her hair.

Her heartbeat increased, her blood flowing hot. When he tipped her head with his hand in her hair she closed her eyes, and felt the whisper of his lips across her eyelids, on her cheek, then settling on her mouth.

The thunder in her ears mingled with the pounding of the sea. Her lips parted and Rolfe deepened the kiss, one hand settling on her breast, the other wandering down her back, finally holding her in an explicit embrace, while the kiss went on and on until she was dizzy with desire.

His hand left her breast as he eased a small space between them, and she felt buttons give way, and trembled. He released her mouth and she gulped in air as his head bent and his mouth touched her skin, wrenching a small cry from her as she felt him push aside her bra, his lips on her breast.

He held her close, his breathing ragged. She arched against him, knowing he was fully aroused, glorying in her ability to do that to him. And in what he was doing to her.

Until he lifted his head and with his lips against her throat, muttered, 'We could visit it tonight...our cave. Shall we go there now?'

Capri stiffened, and he raised his head further, staring down at her face.

He must have seen the sudden doubt and nervous excitement there, mingling with the desire that had nearly overwhelmed her.

His hands fell away from her, leaving her disoriented and cold. 'Don't offer such temptation, Capri, unless you're prepared to follow through. A man can only stand so much.'

Capri took in a sobbing breath, and wrapped her arms about herself, pulling her clothes together. 'I don't mean to tease, Rolfe. It's just that I—' She made a helpless gesture with her hands. 'You must think I'm being stupid.'

'No.' He heaved in a deep breath that came out as a sigh. 'No. I'm trying to understand that things are different for you. I told you I'll wait. Only the waiting isn't getting any easier. I think I want you even more than in those first weeks after we met. At the time I didn't think that was possible.'

'And I want you,' she admitted softly.

'Then what's holding you back?' he demanded.

'I don't know! I—just feel that...that something isn't

right.' It was a lame explanation, she realised wretch-
edly—no explanation at all really.

After a moment he said quietly, 'Has it occurred to
you that maybe it might help restore your memory if we
made love again?'

'Do you truly think so?'

'I have no idea. Nothing else seems to have worked.'
He sounded very fed up. 'And perhaps it might...'

'Might what?'

'Never mind.' His voice was clipped, impatient.

'Perhaps we should visit your cave, after all.'

He said nothing for a long time. 'No,' he ground out
finally. 'Alluring though the thought is, I've no intention
of pressuring you into anything you're not ready for,
Capri. Come on, we'd better get back.'

He took her hand again and they retraced their steps
along the pale, glimmering sand.

When they reached the house Capri collected the
plates from the table, and Rolfe picked up the empty
glasses and the wine bottle, following her inside and to
the kitchen. While she slotted the plates into the dishwasher he rinsed the glasses and dried them.

The light seemed bright in the kitchen. She could almost feel it leaching the colour from her skin as she
turned to Rolfe. 'Thank you.'

He was hanging up the tea-towel. 'You've no need to
thank me.'

'Not just for that,' she said. 'For everything...'

His smile was ironic. 'As I said, you've no need to
thank me.'

There was an awkward silence. Capri decided to
broach something that had nagged at the edge of her
consciousness for weeks. 'Rolfe?'

'Yes?' Rolfe leaned back against the sink counter, folding his arms, his eyes half hidden under lowered lids.

'When I asked about my natural parents, you sort of brushed it aside, as if you didn't want to discuss the subject.'

He looked at her consideringly. 'As I said, you've got enough to cope with.'

'And…?' she pressed him, sure there was more to it.

'Is this important?'

'I don't know. I have a feeling it might be. And I feel that…well, that you're keeping something from me. And I need all the information I can get, if I'm to be well again.'

'All right,' he said reluctantly. 'We…argued about this before you left. That's why you were so determined to travel to Australia. You were trying to find your birth mother.'

It was a small shock. Not her adoptive father. She had been trying to trace her biological mother—the woman who had given birth to her.

'And you didn't want me to?' She looked back at him with grave surprise.

'I thought you should give it some time…'

'Why? And why didn't I agree?'

Rolfe frowned. 'I'm not sure if going over old quarrels is a good idea—'

'Rolfe, I need to know!' With an effort she kept her voice even, reasonable. 'I'm living in…a vacuum. Locked in the dark with no past, groping for memories that I sometimes just touch before they slide away, nothing to hold onto except…you. Relying on you and my mother for every scrap of knowledge about myself.' And Treena hadn't been a great deal of use, her information scattered and often difficult to disentangle. 'You said you wanted to protect me…' she paused as she caught a strange expression on his face, then went on '…but keeping secrets from me isn't going to help.'

His jaw was shut tight. She saw the twitch of a muscle in his cheek. 'Capri, I'm really sorry,' he said at last. 'I've been very selfish—'

'I didn't mean to imply that at all!'

'I know you didn't.' He gave a small, crooked smile. 'But everything you've just said has been coals of fire. I should have insisted on seeking a second opinion as soon as we got back, instead of letting it go for so long.'

'It was my decision,' she reminded him.

'I could have persuaded you to see someone. The truth is,' he said harshly, 'Gabriel was right—it suited me not to have you get better too soon. I've been looking on your—your illness—as a gift, a reprieve of sorts. Because I hoped that if you didn't recall too much too soon, we might get a chance to rebuild our marriage before you remembered what a mess it was.'

CHAPTER THIRTEEN

'OUR marriage...was a mess?' Capri was not really surprised. Without thinking, she added, 'Gabriel said I never meant to come back to you.'

Rolfe's lips tightened and a muscle in his jaw moved convulsively. 'It's possible. I noticed in the hospital that you seemed to have taken off my rings.'

So he'd never really believed that they'd been stolen. 'But...' hope quickened in her breast '...you wanted me back?'

Rolfe stirred, levering himself away from the counter behind him. 'It's getting late, and this isn't a good place for this discussion. Why don't we leave it until tomorrow?'

'No. I...I think I need to sort this out now.'

Rolfe thrust his hands into his pockets and stared at her broodingly. 'At least let's sit somewhere comfortably.'

He led her into the lounge and switched on the side lights that cast a mellow glow, softening the rather stark outlines of the furniture. 'Sit down,' he said, and when she dropped onto a sofa he hesitated a moment before taking a seat on the other side of the gleaming coffee table. He clasped his hands loosely before him, as if he didn't know where to start. Then he took a deep breath. 'After the miscarriage, being on the pill wasn't enough for you. I didn't mind at first that you insisted I use something too. But it became such a ritual...and you

153

were so uptight that I think neither of us found much pleasure in sex.'

Capri shook her head in disbelief. 'Why was I so against having children?'

'I hadn't thought you were. We'd talked of having a family, although not quite so soon. I know you were sometimes careless about taking the pill, so it didn't seem to be vital to you. The issue only became a problem after you lost that pregnancy. Something Sarah said seemed to stick in your mind like a burr.'

'What did she say?'

Rolfe shrugged. 'Just that a miscarriage in the early stages of a pregnancy often means the embryo was imperfect from the start—the technical term for it is a blighted ovum. She meant to comfort us, I guess—persuade us it was for the best. But you worried that something in your biological heritage might have caused the baby to be malformed. And you wouldn't risk another pregnancy until you knew.' He paused. 'That's when you started trying to find out about your natural parents. At first I thought it could be good for you, give you an interest other than fretting about the child we'd lost.'

'But…?' Capri prompted.

'The quest seemed to take over your life. You spent hundreds of dollars in phone calls to Australia, and hours on the computer. The adoption was a closed one where neither set of parents were told much about the other, and Treena didn't want to help—I guess she felt you were rejecting her.'

Capri felt a flash of compunction. Her relationship with Treena had apparently always been fairly difficult.

'At last,' Rolfe said, 'you discovered your natural mother's name, and found an old address of hers in

Australia, but then the trail came to a dead end. There didn't seem to be any more you could do from here.'

'That's when I flew over there,' Capri guessed.

'You were frantic to find her and, given your increasing obsession with the subject, I was afraid of what it might do to you if she didn't want to see you or...if she'd died. I wanted you to wait.'

'And I wouldn't.' She remembered him saying she'd acted on an impulse, refused to allow him to make time to come with her.

'I hoped you'd let me make further enquiries, and give me a week or two to arrange things so I could go along. But when I suggested you shouldn't go off to find her straight away you screamed at me that my work always came before you and our marriage, that I didn't care about you, never had—and a few other things—and I'm afraid in the end I shouted back. Next day when I got home from work, you'd gone.'

'Had I screamed at you before?'

He gave her a rueful look and stood up, paced to the window and turned to face her. 'I don't think we need to go into every row we ever had. It wasn't all on your side. I've done my fair share of shouting now and then.'

Somehow she didn't think he'd have shouted without great provocation. She'd sensed from the first that he had strong feelings, but in her limited experience they'd been kept firmly under control. 'It hasn't been easy being married to me,' she guessed.

His smile was strained. 'I'm no saint myself. And it's had its compensations,' he said. 'Especially lately.'

'Lately? But...' Her eyes lifted to his, then flickered away.

'Sex isn't everything. If we'd realised that sooner, we might have made a more successful marriage. This period of…celibacy has frustrated the hell out of me, but it's also made me aware of so much about you, your personality, that I never knew before. Of course I want to make love to you—at times the wanting has been almost unbearable. But I love you in so many other ways, and more deeply than I ever knew.'

She couldn't speak. The sincerity in his voice, his deep gaze, made her throat close, tears sting at her eyes.

'Back then,' Rolfe said, 'nothing was that clear. You'd think that losing a baby would have brought us closer, but instead we were drifting emotionally further and further apart. I talked to Sarah and she guessed you might have been suffering from a postnatal disorder and should see your regular doctor, but when I suggested it you were furious that I'd even spoken to her. We had a flaming row and…' He shrugged. 'This was months before you left, but we never did make love after that.'

Outside the waves' muted thunder sounded on the shore. Through the darkened glass behind Rolfe, Capri could see the moon, paler and smaller now, looking cold and distant.

'That's when you moved out of our room?'

'I slept in the spare room that night, and the next day you'd moved all my things. It was a clear enough hint. I was pretty fed up myself, and I certainly wasn't going to come begging… I suppose both of us had our pride.'

'You said that we used to…' She felt warmth in her face.

'I know.' He looked briefly at the ceiling. 'I lied by implication. What I told you about us making love on the beach…you seducing me in my study…it was true of the early days of our marriage, Capri.'

But not for the latter months. Was that why she'd

turned to Gabriel, feeling spurned by her husband? Although obviously the fault hadn't been all on his side.

'I didn't want to have to tell you all this,' Rolfe said. 'When you woke in the hospital and looked at me it was—as I already told you—like the first time we met. I know it's been horrible for you, but I've had this feeling that your losing your memory has somehow wiped the slate clean, given us a fresh start—a unique opportunity to do it right this time. And I want that, Capri. I want it very much. These past few weeks I've found myself falling in love with you all over again. And... sometimes I've felt that it's the same for you.'

'Yes.' She admitted it freely. Each day she'd felt the gradual unfurling of the love she must once have felt for him, growing stronger and more certain until now it was in full flower. 'I'm afraid I've not been a very good wife in the past...'

'Don't say that.' He crossed the room and pulled her to her feet. 'We've both made mistakes. I expected too much of you, thinking you were a lot more mature and self-sufficient than you actually were. And for years I'd been tied up with my business, not accustomed to thinking of anyone but myself in my personal life. You called me self-centred and arrogant when we quarrelled, and there's probably some truth in that.' He looked at her frankly. 'Believe me, I want to do better in future. I've told you about the difficult times, when things went wrong, but at first we were happy. You were beautiful and sexy and often funny. And with a sort of street-smart charm that no man could resist. I always loved your laughter. And your occasional moments of childlike naivety, that you seem to have grown out of since the accident, used to surprise me and made me feel tender and protective. I suppose I still felt that way, in spite of my exasperation and disappointment, when I sent a private detective after you to Australia.'

'When you...*what*?'

'I was worried.' She supposed she'd sounded accusing, because he looked slightly discomfited. 'I needed to know you were safe.'

Capri swallowed, a nasty prickling feeling inching along her spine. 'You knew where I was all the time?'

'It wasn't a spying mission, I just wanted to be sure you were all right. He told me you'd travelled around, been to the Northern Territory, looking up official records, and then travelled south. In Adelaide you had several meetings with an older woman and you looked very happy.'

'Still...'

'I understand how you feel. But I felt an obligation to take care of you. I called the detective off when I got that report, guessing you'd found what you were looking for, and knowing you were all right.'

Her mother? She felt a stirring of curiosity but put it aside. This discussion was about Rolfe and herself—their relationship. 'You thought I'd left you.'

'Thea drove you to the airport in your car. She was the one who let me know where you'd gone... And she certainly gained the impression you had no intention of returning. But then, we'd quarrelled the night before and you were still angry with me. I wasn't even sure if she was telling the truth about where you were.'

'That was cruel,' she said, 'leaving without a word. I don't know how I could have done that.'

'Never mind.' He held her hands in his. 'It's all behind us now. Let's concentrate on the future.'

'Yes,' she agreed. Should she mention Gabriel? Did

a new start demand that this too should be brought out in the open?

But as she hesitated Rolfe said, 'You're tired. It's been a long day, and a fairly stressful one.' He drew her closer. 'If I promise to restrain my animal impulses, you might kiss me goodnight, though.'

She lifted her face to him, and he bent and fitted his mouth with great care over hers. One hand slid into her hair as his lips moved in an almost teasing caress. Then he let her go. 'Thank you, Capri. Sleep well.'

She was enormously tired. Lately she hadn't been sleeping all that well, her dreams too often filled with confusing images of darkness and fear that left her with a lingering unease but no clear memory of what they'd been about.

Perhaps emotional exhaustion helped her to stave off the nightmares, because for once she woke refreshed and with a feeling of well-being and anticipation, and no memory of any dreams at all.

Capri supposed her relationship with Rolfe after that could have been called a passionate friendship. She cherished the companionship of their walks, their quiet evenings together. And while he touched her often, and kissed her with frank sensuality, Rolfe seemed to have determined on a gradual, tantalising seduction. Sometimes when he'd brought her to fever pitch he'd withdraw quite suddenly, his eyes gleaming, his cheekbones darkened by a heavy flush, and then he'd give her a hard kiss on her mouth and let her go, with a strange tight smile on his mouth. At times she even wondered if he was bent on some subtle revenge for the frustration she had caused him. But then the smile would change to one that was tender and humorous, and he'd lightly touch her cheek, her hair, and murmur, 'All in good time, my sweet.' Or, 'Don't look so bothered, darling. We have a whole lifetime for this.'

Every day she felt they were growing closer, that soon the barriers would all come down.

She wanted that to happen. Yet there was a tensile joy in this deliberate waiting. And a kind of emotional assurance in knowing that he was willing to let her come to him in her own time, that he wouldn't force the pace.

'Do you know what next Saturday is?' Rolfe asked her as they said goodnight one evening. His hands were on her waist, lightly holding her.

'Next Saturday?' She shook her head blankly.

'The anniversary of our first meeting. I have tickets for the Auckland concert of the Irish dance troupe you liked so much on television. You can dress up for an evening out.'

'Oh, that's nice! I'd love to see them.'

'I knew you would.' On Friday night he came home bearing flowers, a huge mixed bouquet of colours and fragrances, extravagant enough to fill three vases. And on Saturday she spent all afternoon grooming herself and washing and fluffing out her hair, finally dressing in a thin knit gown of silver-threaded sea-green silk that clung to her like a second skin, dipped between her breasts, and showed an expanse of bare thigh through a side slit when she walked. The matching high-heeled shoes made her legs look impossibly long, and she fastened a fine silver chain about her right ankle, emphasising its slimness.

Her courage nearly failed her when she looked in the mirror at her siren-like appearance, but the light in Rolfe's eyes when he saw her made her heart hammer with primitive feminine triumph. She knew very well the outfit was sending an unmistakable message, and all night as she sat beside him, his warm thigh pressing against hers, his hand imprisoning her own, she felt the sexual energy emanating from him. And knew that she was giving off answering vibes, her body shimmering with wanting him.

The dances were spectacular and energetic, with ever-increasing, insistent rhythms. At the climax the bare-chested male star and the sweet innocent female one circled and beat their feet and stared into each other's eyes with erotic fascination. When they finally embraced, the woman's lissom body dramatically, grace-fully curved over the man's supportive arm, Rolfe's hand tightened almost painfully on Capri's, and she didn't dare glance at him, the blood in her body beating in time to the wild but disciplined finale of the massed dancers on stage.

Afterwards Rolfe walked her to the car in silence, and drove home fast, the headlights stabbing through the night, his hands clenched hard on the wheel.

They had hardly got inside, the door shutting softly behind them, when he said, his voice hoarse with effort, his breath lifting her hair, 'Capri, if you don't sleep with me tonight, I think I'll go insane.'

It was dark. They hadn't switched on any lights. Without turning, she said nearly inaudibly, 'I want to.'

Rolfe's arms came around her. His mouth warmed her temple. 'Is that a yes?'

Her hands on the sleeves of his jacket, Capri leaned back, glorying in his strength, and in the shudder that passed through his body. 'Yes.'

She felt the huge breath that he hauled into his lungs and then let out. 'Oh, thank God!'

She was picked up and carried through the darkness, and he kicked open the door of her room and slammed it again with his foot.

The curtains were open, the stars falling through the sky outside, and in the distance faint moving glimmers of white split the black satin of the sea. He put her on her feet by the bed and held her close and kissed her, long and passionate and sweet. His hands moulded her bare shoulders and drifted down her back and opened the zip, his fingers caressing her spine. Then he released her mouth, and carefully lifted the dress away from her shoulders, slid it down her arms and let it pool at her feet. It wasn't a dress that she could wear with a bra, and she made an instinctive move to cover her breasts, but stopped herself and instead lifted her hands to push his jacket off.

Rolfe smiled and helped her, before he wrenched off his tie and began unbuttoning his shirt while she stepped out of her shoes. Then she took his wrists and whispered, 'Let me.'

She undid the cuffs, fumbling a little, and then turned her attention to the front of the shirt, flipping each button open. He put his hands on her hips just above the scanty bikini briefs she wore, and brought her closer so that she felt the hardness of his arousal, and heat coursed through all her bones.

She eased the shirt from his shoulders, letting her hands glide down his arms, and he momentarily released his hold on her to get rid of the garment.

'You have beautiful breasts,' he told her, and ran his hands up over her waist to touch them, making her close her eyes, her head going back as she drew in a sharp breath of pleasure. 'You're beautiful all over.'

She opened her eyes, found his blazing with need. 'So are you.'

Her hands fumbled at his belt, and he gave a short laugh and said, 'Wait.'

He sat on the bed to tug off his shoes and socks, and then lay back, pulling her on top of him. 'Okay, now you can have your wicked way with me.'

But he made it difficult by holding her under her arms and kissing her breasts as she lay above him, finally taking one eager tip into his mouth, setting up sensations so overwhelming that she moaned and involuntarily moved, pressing her body down on his.

Rolfe's mouth left her, and he gave a gasping grunt and flipped her over onto her back, then briefly released her to shuck off the rest of his clothing.

Capri found herself shivering with anticipation, with half-understood need. 'Rolfe—' She groped for him in the darkness, a shadowy, bulky male form.

'I'm here. I never want to be anywhere else.' He settled alongside her, skin to skin, and began a teasing, erotic survey of her body with the tips of his fingers, lighting tiny fires all over her. He kissed her, and she returned the kiss fervently, still shivering.

'Are you cold?' he asked, making to pull the cover over them.

'No. No, not cold…I don't know. Nervous, I guess,' she confessed. 'But don't stop!' as his fingers stilled. 'Don't stop. It's just…I suppose it's like the first time. Because I can't remember any other…'

'I don't think I could stop,' Rolfe said soberly. 'I want you so much I think I'll die if I have to wait another day.'

'I feel the same,' she told him, reaching for him,

touching him in turn, rather shyly. 'I feel as if I've waited all my life for this.'

'My darling girl! Don't be afraid, there's no need. I'll make this good for you.' He leaned over her and kissed her again, on her mouth, and then her breasts, her belly, thighs, and after he'd gently removed the last flimsy barrier she sighed as he breathed in her scent and kissed her even more intimately.

She was shaking, out of her mind with pleasure, and with knowing that he too was approaching the edge, passionately returning his kisses, her hands exploring him, her body pressing against his until he eased himself over her and smoothed the tumbled hair back from her face and she cried out to him with fierce wanting, 'Now! Oh, please...I want you now!'

They were past tenderness, and her cry galvanised him to a potent, silent answer. She was clutching at him, her eyes demanding his response, her body waiting, ready, yearning for him. She saw his eyes light with an answering fire, and then felt him touch her, hard and hot and seeking entry, and she opened to him fearlessly, every nerve on tenterhooks, wanting him as she knew she'd never wanted anything in her entire life.

He slid into her, deep and sure and commanding— and instantly her body was seared with shocking, tearing pain, her throat ripped by an unwilling scream. She opened her eyes wide with panic, but everything was black, her head buzzing, and her eyelids fluttered closed again as she slid into swirling darkness.

'Capri? My God, what happened? *Capri?*'

She was cold, her senses swimming, the aftermath of pain still aching deep inside her. Her eyes were tightly shut against it.

'Capri!' She felt Rolfe's hands on her shoulders, and then they were gone and she heard the rasp of the curtains being pulled across.

Light struck her eyes and she flinched. He'd turned on the bedside lamp.

'I hurt you,' he was saying, and she felt the bed depress beside her, his hand on her thigh. 'I'm so sorry, darling! It never occurred to me that after all this time it might not be easy for you.'

She opened her eyes, disoriented and dizzy, and found him looking stricken, white-faced, his eyes anxious. 'It's all right,' she managed to murmur. 'Not your fault.'

'I should have been more careful. God, I'm sorry!'

'I know.' She tried to think, to frame words. This was a nightmare. 'I...' She fumbled for the sheet, wanting to cover herself.

He saw what she was trying to do, and bent to gather the bedclothes for her, then suddenly went utterly still, staring down at her bare thighs. 'Capri...when was your last period?'

'A week ago.' She blinked, attempted to grab the sheet from him, but he wouldn't let go. His cheeks gaunt, his already pale skin turning sallow, he said hoarsely, 'Those damned doctors missed something after the accident! Did they ever give you an internal examination?'

'I don't think so. It wasn't necessary. Rolfe—'

A curse exploded from his lips. 'There's something wrong. I'll call Sarah.'

He dropped the sheet over her and grabbed the bedside phone.

'No!' she said. 'Rolfe—'

'We need a doctor!' He began stabbing at the buttons.

'No, Rolfe, we—I don't.' She winced, leaning over to stop him, cutting the connection. 'Put it down.'

He wrenched the receiver away. 'You don't understand, darling,' he said agitatedly. 'You're bleeding!'

She swallowed. 'I know.' Stubbornly she gripped his wrist. 'There's a reason for that.'

'Of course there's a *reason*—and we need to find out what it is! It can't be normal.'

'But it is!' she insisted, against the unreal sensations that bombarded her. She had a peculiar feeling that she was floating somewhere in a strange space, and her voice didn't seem to belong to her. 'It's perfectly normal, Rolfe, in the…circumstances.'

'What circumstances?' he asked impatiently, glancing up from trying to dial through again. 'There can't be—'

She held his eyes, willing him to listen. To believe the unbelievable. 'You don't understand, Rolfe. I'm…I *was*…a virgin.'

CHAPTER FOURTEEN

ROLFE didn't move for a long, long second. His hand dropped, still clutching the phone. 'For God's sake, Capri, you were my wife for two years—and we've been sleeping together longer than that!' His eyes narrowed, blazed. 'You weren't a virgin when we met, let alone when you left me! What the hell are you trying to pull now?'

She supposed she should have expected anger. He'd been wrenched from desire to disaster and was totally at sea. 'I'm not—I never did try to cheat you, Rolfe. Not in any way.' She plucked at the sheet, trying to cover her breasts, acutely conscious of her nakedness, and of his. 'Please,' she said huskily, 'put down the phone and let me explain. I promise you I don't need medical attention. But I would like to get some clothes on. And I think you should too.'

Slowly he replaced the receiver and stood up, staring at her as if he'd never seen her before, while his expression changed from baffled anger to appalled comprehension and then stunned disbelief.

He turned and picked up his discarded clothes, glanced at her once more, and strode through the bathroom to his own bedroom.

She got up, shivering, and found some tissues to wipe her thighs. Clumsily she hunted for and pulled on a pair of panties and an enveloping towelling robe, tying the belt tightly. The air temperature was too warm for such a heavy garment but the cosy fabric was somehow comforting. She'd have liked a shower, but didn't want to run into Rolfe in the bathroom.

She was sitting on the bed staring numbly at the drawn curtains when he tapped on the door.

'Come in,' she called automatically.

He carried a glass of some amber liquid and a steaming cup. 'I thought you might like a hot drink,' he said. 'It's tea with sugar. I guess you're suffering from shock.'

She took the cup. 'Thank you. I'm not the only one, am I?'

His mouth made an effort at some kind of smile. 'Right.' He lifted the glass and tossed off the contents. 'Are you sure you're all right? Physically.'

'Yes. It's…good of you to be concerned. I appreciate that.' Her voice was stilted as she made the formal little speech.

He stood before the closed curtains, staring at her as she sipped the hot, sweet tea.

'You're very certain,' he said, 'about your facts. One fact, anyway.'

'Yes.' She looked down into the cup, and felt herself trembling.

'Your memory's returned.' It was more of a statement than a question.

'Yes.' It had crashed in on her all at once, like a gigantic tidal wave, overwhelming her with its force. She remembered everything, right up to the rending, hair-raising sounds of tearing metal as the train was pushed off the track and half into the river, sounds mingling with the screams of the terrified passengers, the injured, the dying. She closed her eyes.

When she opened them Rolfe was still looking at her, his eyes reflecting much of her own dazed incredulity at what had happened to them. Between them.

He shook his head as if to clear it, and said, his voice so flat and emotionless she knew he was keeping it that way with a superhuman effort of will, 'Then...who the hell are you?'

CHAPTER FIFTEEN

'I'M…' Her voice was husky, barely audible. 'I'm Francesca Ryan—Capri's twin.'

'Twin.' Tonelessly he repeated the word as if it meant nothing, could mean nothing. 'This is…incredible.'

'I know.' She still felt incredulous herself. And disoriented—and afraid. 'Capri found me, you see. She'd traced our birth mother and discovered that she'd had twins, but we'd been adopted by different families.'

He frowned sceptically. 'Surely that wouldn't have been allowed, even twenty years ago.'

'It should never have happened. Capri was told when she went to the authorities and asked about me that it *couldn't* have happened. There's going to be an inquiry into the departmental records.'

'How do you know all this?'

'Capri told me.'

He shook his head in disbelief. 'Capri never knew she had a twin.'

'Neither did I. Our mother has a husband, children…other children. When Capri found her, she asked for time to break the news to them and let them get used to the idea before she introduced their new half-sister. Capri promised, and then she went looking for me. She was very excited to find me…I was too. It was the most peculiar feeling, seeing myself in a stranger's face. And yet we had so many things in common—likes and dislikes, our taste in music, even gestures, and our voices…'

'I've sometimes thought your accent…Capri's accent—was slightly different since the accident. I put it down to your—her—having spent time back in Australia so recently.' He was looking at her as though he couldn't take his eyes off her. 'You know more about New Zealand than you'd have got from geography lessons.'

He was still faintly suspicious. She couldn't blame him, given the fantastic turn of events. 'My father—my adoptive father, I mean—is a computer engineer specialising in dairy machinery. We spent a year in New Zealand when I was still at school while he helped set up a new factory complex in the north. Then we went back to Australia, and now my parents live just outside Gosford with my younger brother. They adopted me because they had three boys and there hadn't been a girl in my father's family for three generations—and my mother desperately wanted a girl.'

'You'll want to get in touch.'

'Yes.' But not now. There were things she had to say to this man first. 'Capri showed me photographs of you, and her adoptive family, and of this house. She'd brought them along to show her—our—mother. To show any family she found, I suppose. We were looking through them on the train when…when it crashed. That's why your face was familiar when I came to in the hospital, and how I knew your name. And why I recognised the house when you brought me here. Those photographs would have been the last thing I saw. She'd taken them out of her bag, and it was open on the seat between us.'

He nodded. His lips compressed. 'How was she?'

Francesca swallowed. She felt as though her heart was being torn apart inside her. 'She was thrilled and happy that she'd found me—and found our mother. We had a lot of fun swapping childhood stories, giggling like a couple of schoolgirls, trying to catch up on the years we'd been apart, reliving a childhood that we'd never had together. She...spoke of you.' Looking down, Francesca twisted the empty cup in her hands, trying to hide the pain that threatened to overwhelm her. 'She said you were handsome and successful and willing to give her anything.' And sexy, she'd said, laughing and looking saucy and coy. There'd been no mention of Gabriel. According to Capri everything in her particular garden of Eden was rosy. She hadn't wanted to admit to her new-found family that she might have failed at anything, or been less than honourable, that her life was not utterly perfect.

'I...' Rolfe cleared his throat. 'I tried. To give her everything she wanted. But she was...'

'Needy. I know. Even in the short time I knew her, I felt that in her. You would have been good for her, you'd have...cared for her. I'm sure she loved you.' As much as she could love anyone, without ever quite trusting them to love her back... 'I think she would have come home to you.'

But first, perhaps, she'd have wanted to punish him, hurt him, let him worry about her. Because she'd been wilful and difficult and not quite mature. And afraid that no one truly loved her.

'Thank you,' Rolfe said formally.

Her throat ached. 'I liked her. She was the other half of myself, that I hadn't known existed. But I think that all her life she'd felt incomplete in a way I never had.'

'Yes.' The word came out on a breath, a sigh.

'She said she'd always known deep down that something was missing. She'd never had the feeling of belonging. Finding me was like...suddenly being whole. It meant more to her than it did to me, because I'd been lucky. I love my family dearly, and I know they couldn't have loved me more if I'd been their natural daughter. And I know Treena tried her best, but Capri hadn't ever really got over her parents' divorce. I don't think she felt safe after that—she spent her life looking for a security that no one could have given her.' Raising her eyes, she said steadily, 'It wasn't your fault, Rolfe. It was her own sense of incompleteness and insecurity that drove her…'

'Into Gabriel Blake's arms,' he said grimly.

For a long moment Francesca was silent. 'You knew they were lovers.'

'I wasn't sure how far it had gone. Whether she was merely flirting with the idea of infidelity, or trying to capture my attention or…if she was genuinely in love with him. But yes, of course I knew she was seeing him. When she disappeared I thought maybe she'd gone to him, that Thea was covering for her when she said Capri was headed for Australia. Then Gabriel came looking for her.' He smiled bitterly. 'I suppose in his way he loved Capri.'

'He wouldn't have held her either, Rolfe. She didn't even know what she was searching for, but it wasn't a man.'

Rolfe nodded. He looked away, then steadily back at her, his eyes sombre. 'She's dead, isn't she?'

Tears filled her eyes and scalded her cheeks. She had to gulp them back, trying to steady her voice. 'We were going to see my family. My adoptive family, I mean. We planned to surprise them—like children. That's how Capri had got me to meet her in Sydney…with a mysterious phone call, asking me to meet someone I'd be pleased to see, in a hotel bar. I wondered if it was some kind of new marketing ploy at first. Or even something sinister. But in a public place, and she was so insistent…I couldn't help being intrigued. And when I walked in and saw her…'

'You must have been stunned.'

Francesca managed to lift a hand to wipe away the tears. 'Putting it mildly.' Straightening her shoulders, she said quietly, 'I don't think she ever knew what happened. There was a horrendous noise and everything rocked over to one side. I blacked out for—I don't know, maybe a couple of minutes—and when I came to she was lying across me, bleeding… As soon as I moved her I knew…there was no hope for her. She died in my arms.'

Rolfe turned abruptly, presenting his back to her, his head bowed onto one raised hand.

'I'm so sorry,' she whispered. 'About everything.' There was a huge ache in her chest, partly for Capri, her sister, and partly for Rolfe in his bereavement. And also for herself, for the shining future that she'd glimpsed so briefly, and that now was cruelly snatched away.

She wanted to go to him, hurl herself into his arms and cry out that she loved him, needed him, wanted to stay with him for ever, to comfort him in his loss.

Because she had come to love him over the past weeks, and all the while he hadn't known who she really was. When he'd shown her such patience and tenderness and compassion, and desire and love and even anger, he'd been caught in an illusion, believing she was his beloved, his wife, the woman he had planned to spend his life loving.

It wasn't her place to offer the comfort of her arms, or take comfort from his. She was a stranger to him, an unwitting impostor who didn't belong in his bed, in his home, in his life...

'How did you get out?' Rolfe asked, his voice muffled.

'I'm not sure. There were people climbing all over us, seats had been wrenched from the floor, luggage and other things were still falling, the carriage hadn't stopped moving and there was water coming in...' She stopped, shivering with remembered horror. 'Someone grabbed me, tried to help me out of a broken window, and then I think the carriage slid further and maybe something cracked me on the head. Because that's all I remember until I woke up in the hospital...and you were there.'

He was standing now as she had first seen him, his shoulders hunched and his hands in his pockets, with his back to her. He said hoarsely, 'You were found on the riverbank with other passengers who had got out somehow. When Capri's bag was recovered among the stuff that had floated downriver, the hospital authorities matched the passport and the other photos with you, and having done that, no one would think to look further.'

Their birth mother wouldn't have known they were on the train. Even if she'd seen the list of those killed, Capri's name wouldn't have been there.

Not Capri's name. But Francesca's...

'I believe,' she said slowly, 'my adoptive parents may have identified her as me.'

Rolfe was silent for a moment. 'God, yes,' he said, and swung round to look at her, his face grey. 'You'd better get hold of them.'

CHAPTER SIXTEEN

'FRAN! Phone!'

Her younger brother's shout brought Francesca hurrying inside, stripping off the gardening gloves she wore, and leaving her shoes on the porch. 'Who is it?'

Shayne shrugged angular shoulders. 'How would I know? One of your boyfriends, I guess.' He handed over the receiver.

Fran gave him a reproving look. Boyfriends were a thing of the past, ever since she'd returned home, shattered and pale, to a tumultuous, tearful welcome from a family who had thought her gone for ever. And she'd stayed, instead of returning to her flat in Sydney, because there were unseen wounds that still had not healed. 'Hello?'

'It's Rolfe.' His voice was clipped and sounded almost cold. 'I wondered if I could...see you. I'm in Gosford.'

'Rolfe!' Her hand was suddenly clammy on the receiver. She hadn't seen him or spoken to him since the day nine months ago when she'd stood with her family and Capri's beside the gravestone that now bore her sister's name in the local cemetery, where Rolfe and Treena and the twins' natural mother had agreed that her troubled soul should remain at rest. Now and then Fran placed a bouquet of flowers there, and cried a little for the sister she had never really known. Had Rolfe been there again today?

'Will you come?' he said abruptly.

And she replied, 'Of course.' She could no more refuse him than she could have refused to breathe.

He took her to a bar, and ordered dry white wine, then hesitated. 'Is that right?'

Capri had liked dry white; he'd never asked before. Fran nodded. She and her sister had been amazed at the convergence of their tastes after a lifetime apart. She'd since done some reading about twins and realised the phenomenon wasn't uncommon.

She was tongue-tied, and she thought Rolfe felt awkward too. He'd ordered a beer for himself, and didn't speak until it was nearly finished. 'How are you?' he said.

'You already asked. I told you—'

'You said you were fine. *Are* you, really?'

'Yes.' But she looked down, avoiding his eyes, because there was a pain around her heart that wouldn't go away, despite her family's astonished, grateful love and care, despite her return to the work she loved as an illustrator for nature magazines. On the surface her life appeared to have returned to normal following the traumatic events after the train crash. But the experience had profoundly altered her; she knew she wasn't the same and never would be.

There would never again be a day when she didn't recall that for a few short months Rolfe had thought he loved her—never a day when she didn't remember his smile, or the touch of his hand, or the passion of his kisses, when she didn't piercingly feel the loss of a happiness that had not been rightfully hers.

The books she'd read didn't say much about twins loving the same man.

Rolfe was drawing circles on the table with his glass.

'I'm glad…' he said, his voice low and hoarse, '…that you've recovered.'

She quelled a bitter smile at that. 'Did you…?' She hesitated. 'Have you been to the cemetery?'

'Yesterday.' He cleared his throat. 'To say a final goodbye to the past. I…I don't suppose you want her rings? As her sister…'

'No. No, but thank you for thinking of it.' Capri's wedding and engagement rings had been routinely removed for safekeeping by the police before Francesca's family had mistakenly identified her as their own daughter. Offered the jewellery, Fran's parents had assumed some mistake, and the rings had stayed with the police until Rolfe claimed them.

Francesca picked up her glass and put it down again without drinking. 'Perhaps Treena…or Venetia…?' she suggested.

He nodded. 'I'll ask. If there's anything you'd like as a keepsake…I think she'd want you to have something.'

'Thank you. I'd like that.'

A strained silence fell. Fran broke it finally. 'Are you…getting over it?'

'I am over it, if you mean Capri's death. At least as much as one does get over the death of someone you've been close to. It's taken months to come to terms with what really happened. For a while I felt numbed, in an emotional vacuum. Then everything became totally confused and I was riding an emotional see-saw. Now—it's all over. I've mourned her…and our marriage. I needed to do that before…well, before I could move on.'

'I'm glad you feel you *can* move on. She wouldn't have wanted anything else for you.'

'I hope you're right.' He stared at his drink, then quickly lifted it and gulped some down. 'What about you? Have you been able to pick up the threads of your life, Francesca? Are you...over it?'

Fran didn't quite understand the look he gave her. She shrugged. Could she tell him she was in limbo, that she missed him with a deep, abiding ache that never went away, that the months she'd spent with him had become a part of her life that would be with her until death—that had altered her for ever? That every man she met would be measured against him, and she couldn't make herself believe there would ever be a man to take his place in her heart, her life?

She wouldn't burden him with that. She said, 'We both needed time to adjust.'

'Yes. It's been incredibly difficult sorting out my feelings for...for Capri, and for you.'

He'd thought they were one and the same. 'I know.' It wasn't something that could be done overnight. Or even in a matter of weeks. Discovering his wife was dead would have been traumatic enough for any man. Rolfe had also had to cope with a complex nightmare of mistaken identity and false assumptions—and guilt, she guessed. Guilt that he'd taken the wrong woman into his home and cared for her, wooed her, made love to her, while his real wife, his true love, was lying in a grave marked with someone else's name.

She drank some more wine and replaced her half-empty glass on the table. 'It must have been hard for you, knowing she's...she was dead all along, and you were...you thought...'

'I thought that I was falling in love with her all over again. But I wasn't. I was falling in love with you.'

Francesca's heart stopped. She felt it. Then it took up its beat, faster. She couldn't move, could scarcely breathe.

'I didn't realise of course, at the time.' He was silent for a while, then drew an audible breath. 'Before she went away, when I knew Capri was seeing Gabriel Blake...' his shoulders hunched '...I didn't know if she was sleeping with him, and it didn't seem to matter all that much, although I knew it should. I hadn't been able to give her whatever it was she wanted from me. Maybe he could. Or maybe she was trying to punish me for not caring enough, or hoping I'd find out about the affair and make an effort to win her back, give her the attention she craved so badly.' He moved the glass again, not looking up. 'I should have been jealous, but I just felt saddened that we seemed to have lost whatever it was that brought us together—that we'd thought we'd have for ever. I knew our marriage was dying before she left. And then, from the time I brought you home—thinking you were her—everything changed. Life was new and exciting. Love was possible after all. I realised—I thought—that I did love my wife, and I wanted desperately to repair my marriage. I was overhelmingly grateful for the second chance.'

Francesca tensed, her whole being concentrated on him, on what he was saying.

He looked up at last, and she saw pain in his eyes. 'When I came upon you...holding hands with Gabriel...quite simply I wanted to kill him. And afterwards take you to bed and leave my mark on you in the most primitive way...' He glanced down again. 'I should never have allowed myself near you while I was feeling like that. I horrified myself that day, treating you the way I did.'

Fran swallowed, unable to speak. This was a revelation of hope that she was afraid to grasp at too greedily, too quickly. She could scarcely take in what he was saying—what she thought he was saying.

'You don't want to listen to my confessions. My apologies for asking you to,' Rolfe said roughly. 'I should have stayed away. I suppose this is in the worst of taste. After what I did to you, I guess you probably never wanted to see me again.'

'Rolfe...' she whispered, her voice refusing to work properly.

Looking up, he gave her a smile that wrenched at her heart. 'I have no right to do this to you. It's not your problem. You...go on with your life, Francesca,' he said. 'This is too complicated. I'll get out of here, never bother you again. Forget I said anything. It was stupid of me.'

He moved as though ready to leave, to walk away from her, and she reached out and placed both her hands over his. 'Rolfe,' she said. 'Please.'

He sucked in a breath, closing his eyes. 'Don't touch me,' he said, 'Fran...Francesca. Don't.'

Her name sounded so sweet on his lips. 'You do know I'm Fran,' she said quietly, so quietly. 'You know that.'

'Of course I know it!' He looked at her then, eyes blazing. 'I know...you're not your sister.' He dragged another harsh breath inward. 'Somewhere deep inside I think I knew it from the moment I laid eyes on you.'

'You said it was like the first time you met her.'

'Yes,' he agreed heavily. 'And yet it was always different. *You* were always different. The face was hers, but...the person behind the face...you were serene and very grown-up and so...giving. Although you were nervous of making love, and I didn't understand why until...well, you know. I was both intrigued and exasperated by your caution and—what I know now was inexperience, the natural fear of the unknown. And I was intensely frustrated, of course. But that night when you let me make love to you at last, there was something about knowing that you didn't remember any other time…any other man. I wanted to cherish you, love you, waken you to what lovemaking between a man and woman could be when they really love each other as I loved you. And I'd give anything…to change the way it ended. I wish to God I'd realised earlier…'

She flushed, but refused to look away. And after a moment he did, his gaze fixing on their hands. 'Capri was always volatile, unpredictable. Part of her charm— she had an abundance of that—but…wearing. I did love her in the beginning—even, in a way, to the end. But not in the way I love you. After the first few months I had to work at it, remind myself that I'd taken her for better or worse. There were times when I remembered why I'd fallen in love with her, when it was almost like those early, dizzying weeks after we first met. We might have made it. I'd hoped we would, that something was still salvageable. After the accident I began to be certain that I'd love her for ever, that we did after all have something deep and enduring and nothing could erase it from my heart, my life. Only that wasn't Capri. It was you. Francesca.'

He lifted his head and looked at her, and she gazed back at him with clear green eyes and said simply, 'I'm in love with you, Rolfe. I think I have been since the first moment I opened my eyes and saw you. And I've been so afraid that…that you never really wanted *me* at all.'

His hands turned on the table and gripped hers. 'I don't think I dare believe this,' he muttered.

'It's true. I love you and I didn't know how I was going to live the rest of my life without you.' She sucked her lower lip briefly. 'Please, can we go someplace where you can hold me?'

CHAPTER SEVENTEEN

'TO HAVE and to hold,' the minister intoned. 'From this day forward...'

Francesca repeated the words, her voice steady and clear. Minutes later Rolfe slid a gleaming new gold ring on her finger and soon afterwards bent to kiss her.

She kissed him back, a kiss full of sweetness and promise. He'd waited for three months after asking her to marry him—determined, he said, to do the thing properly, to give her the courtship she'd missed out on when they'd got things so muddled the first time. And also, she suspected, to reassure her anxious parents that she was in no way a substitute for the wife he had lost.

Fran's natural mother was there too, wiping tears away. Although they shared a unique bond and Fran had grown fond of her and made friends with her husband and other children, this woman who had once been a troubled, frightened, pregnant teenager from a strict Italian background would never replace the mother who had loved her all her life.

Her adoptive family had opened its collective heart to Rolfe, and although he was taking her home with him she knew there would be plenty of visiting back and forth across the Tasman. Shayne had already booked his next school holiday with them.

In a luxury Sydney hotel that night, Rolfe ordered champagne and sandwiches, and while she showered he flipped off all the lights but one, and was waiting for her when she returned wearing a sliver of white satin that skimmed her breasts and her hips.

'This time,' he promised, 'I'll be far more careful. I swear I'll give you nothing but pleasure. And you must tell me if there's anything you don't like.' He touched her hair, her shoulder, laid his fingers against her breast, and palmed the beat of her heart. Then he kissed her gently, lingeringly and reluctantly withdrew. 'My turn in the bathroom. I won't be long.'

She slipped under the bedcovers and listened to him in the shower, then got out of the bed and padded across the room. He was stepping out of the shower cubicle when she surprised him.

Water dripped down his body—a magnificent body, she thought, inspecting it. Growing more so by the minute.

'Fran?' He grabbed a towel. 'Something wrong?'

Slowly she shook her head. 'No. Not that I can see.' She took the towel from him and without hurry ran it over his chest.

Rolfe's eyes glittered and he snatched the towel from her, giving himself a cursory wipe over. 'If you don't want to be ravished right here,' he suggested, 'you'd better go back to bed.'

'Only if you promise to ravish me there,' she answered, her cheeks flushed, her eyes smiling.

He made a choked sound and picked her up in his strong arms, shouldering his way out from the steamy room to the bedroom with its king-size bed. 'I thought you'd be scared,' he said, 'after the last time.'

'Why should I be scared of you?'

He lay down on the bed with her, his naked, still damp body hot through the cool satin that covered hers. 'I hurt you so much...have you forgotten?'

'I haven't forgotten. And I haven't forgotten how you made love to me before that…as though it was my first time…even while you thought it wasn't. I haven't forgotten your patience, and your gentleness, and your passion… I never wanted to forget it, not in all those months when I thought it was all I was ever going to have of you. I want it all over again, Rolfe. I want you, to have and to hold, from this day forward…'

'As I want you,' he answered. 'But I'm going to make this slow and gentle and wonderful for you, my darling. Something so good you'll remember it for ever.'

He kept the promise—his mouth, his fingers, his body working tender magic that weaved a spell of delight, spiralling higher and higher, a gradual seduction of the senses, until she sighed into his mouth, *'Now.'*

This time there was no pain, only the most exquisite of pleasures, and a feeling of utter completeness, a mysterious fusion of two into one. And then the dazzling, erotic, all-consuming dark whirlwind shot with stars, the ultimate expression of love between man and woman that took them both beyond reality into a world of utter sensation.

She drifted down from the heights they'd shared, her head against his shoulder, his hand stroking her back.

'You're right,' she whispered, turning her head to touch his salty skin with her lips. 'This is a memory that I'll cherish as long as I live.'

'And so will I,' he told her soberly, stroking her hair away from her forehead with gentle fingers. 'I should tell you I fully intend to spend the rest of my life making memories just like it. Memories that neither of us will ever lose.'

Francesca smiled dreamily into the darkness. 'I know,' she said with utter certainty, 'I never will.'

MILLS & BOON®

Next Month's Romance Titles

♡

Each month you can choose from a wide variety of romance novels from Mills & Boon®. Below are the new titles to look out for next month from the Presents™ and Enchanted™ series.

Presents™

ONE NIGHT IN HIS ARMS	Penny Jordan
FATHERHOOD FEVER!	Emma Darcy
THE BRIDAL SUITE	Sandra Marton
HE'S MY HUSBAND!	Lindsay Armstrong
MARRIAGE UNDER SUSPICION	Sara Craven
REMARRIED IN HASTE	Sandra Field
THE HUSBAND CONTRACT	Kathleen O'Brien
THE BOSS'S MISTRESS	Kathryn Ross

Enchanted™

A MOST ELIGIBLE BACHELOR	Jessica Steele
THE PLAYBOY ASSIGNMENT	Leigh Michaels
HIS LITTLE GIRL	Liz Fielding
WANTED: PERFECT WIFE	Barbara McMahon
BRIDE BY FRIDAY	Trisha David
WEDDING BELLS	Patricia Knoll
HER MISTLETOE HUSBAND	Renee Roszel
A DAD FOR DANIEL	Janelle Denison

On sale from 6th November 1998

H1 9810

Available at most branches of WH Smith, Tesco, Asda, Martins, Borders and all good paperback bookshops

Your Special
Christmas
Gift

Three romance novels from Mills & Boon® to
unwind with at your leisure—
and a luxurious Le Jardin bath gelée to pamper
you and gently wash your cares away.

for just £5.99

Featuring
Carole Mortimer—Married by Christmas
Betty Neels—A Winter Love Story
Jo Leigh—One Wicked Night

MILLS & BOON®

Makes your Christmas time special

Available from 23rd October 1998

CHRISTMAS
Affairs

MORE THAN JUST KISSES UNDER THE MISTLETOE...

Enjoy three sparkling seasonal romances by your
favourite authors from

MILLS & BOON®
Presents™

HELEN BIANCHIN
For Anique, the season of goodwill has become...
The Seduction Season

SANDRA MARTON
Can Santa weave a spot of Christmas magic for Nick
and Holly in... *A Miracle on Christmas Eve?*

SHARON KENDRICK
Will Aleck and Clemmie have a... *Yuletide Reunion?*

MILLS & BOON®
Makes any time special™

Available from 6th November 1998

Jennifer
BLAKE

KANE

Down in Louisiana, family comes first.
That's the rule the Benedicts live by.
So when a beautiful redhead starts paying a little
too much attention to Kane Benedict's grandfather,
Kane decides to find out what her *real* motives are.

*"Blake's style is as steamy as a still July night...as overwhelming
hot as Cajun spice."*

—Chicago Times

x

1-55166-429-1
AVAILABLE IN PAPERBACK
FROM OCTOBER, 1998

FIND THE FRUIT!

How would you like to win a year's supply of Mills & Boon® Books—FREE! Well, if you know your fruit, then you're already one step ahead when it comes to completing this competition, because all the answers are fruit! Simply decipher the code to find the names of ten fruit, complete the coupon overleaf and send it to us by 30th April 1999. The first five correct entries will each win a year's subscription to the Mills & Boon series of their choice. What could be easier?

A	B	C	D	E	F	G	H	I
15					20			
J	**K**	**L**	**M**	**N**	**O**	**P**	**Q**	**R**
	25						5	
S	**T**	**U**	**V**	**W**	**X**	**Y**	**Z**	
			10					

4	19	15	17	22

15	10	3	17	15	18	3

2	19	17	8	15	6	23	2	19

4	19	15	6

4	26	9	1

7	8	6	15	11	16	19	6	6	13

3	6	15	2	21	19

15	4	4	26	19

1	15	2	21	3

16	15	2	15	2	15

C8J

Please turn over for details of how to enter ➜

HOW TO ENTER

There are ten coded words listed overleaf, which when decoded each spell the name of a fruit. There is also a grid which contains each letter of the alphabet and a number has been provided under some of the letters. All you have to do, is complete the grid, by working out which number corresponds with each letter of the alphabet. When you have done this, you will be able to decipher the coded words to discover the names of the ten fruit! As you decipher each code, write the name of the fruit in the space provided, then fill in the coupon below, pop this page into an envelope and post it today. Don't forget you could win a year's supply of Mills & Boon® Books—you don't even need to pay for a stamp!

Mills & Boon Find the Fruit Competition
FREEPOST CN81, Croydon, Surrey, CR9 3WZ
EIRE readers: (please affix stamp) PO Box 4546, Dublin 24.

Please tick the series you would like to receive if you are one of the lucky winners
Presents™ ❏ Enchanted™ ❏ Medical Romance™ ❏
Historical Romance™ ❏ Temptation® ❏

Are you a Reader Service™ subscriber? Yes ❏ No ❏

Ms/Mrs/Miss/Mr ....Initials ....
(BLOCK CAPITALS PLEASE)

Surname...

Address ....

....

....Postcode..........................

(I am over 18 years of age)   C8J·

Subscription prizes are for 4 books a month for 12 months. Closing date for entries is 30th April 1999. One entry per household. Competition open to residents of the UK and Ireland only. As a result of this application, you may receive further offers from Harlequin Mills & Boon and other carefully selected companies. If you would prefer not to share in this opportunity please write to The Data Manager, P.O. Box 236, Croydon, Surrey CR9 3RU.
Mills & Boon is a registered trademark owned by Harlequin Mills & Boon Limited.